But the way Elijah's blood simmered as he stood this close to Camden, breathing in the acrid scent of medicinal soap wafting off his skin, Elijah didn't think safe was the right word to describe their current status. Slightly intoxicated by the desire Elijah knew he shouldn't have for a man he shouldn't want, Elijah paused a second to let his gaze slide up and down Camden's lean body. A moment was all it took to remember how glorious Camden was in nothing but his bare skin, and for Elijah to recognize the real threat Camden was. They might have been safe from Camden's enemies, but being safe from each other was another matter altogether.

WELCOME TO

⟳REAMSPUN DESIRES

Dear Reader,

Love is the dream. It dazzles us, makes us stronger, and brings us to our knees. Dreamspun Desires tell stories of love featuring your favorite heartwarming heroes, captivating plots, and exotic locations. Stories that make your breath catch and your imagination soar.

In the pages of these wonderful love stories, readers can escape to a world where love conquers all, the tenderness of a first kiss sweeps you away, and your heart pounds at the sight of the one you love.

When you put it all together, you find romance in its truest form.

Love always finds a way.

Elizabeth North

Executive Director
Dreamspinner Press

LaQuette

UNDER HIS
PROTECTION

DREAMSPUN DESIRES

PUBLISHED BY

DREAMSPINNER
PRESS

Published by
DREAMSPINNER PRESS

5032 Capital Circle SW, Suite 2, PMB# 279,
Tallahassee, FL 32305-7886 USA
www.dreamspinnerpress.com

This is a work of fiction. Names, characters, places, and incidents either
are the product of author imagination or are used fictitiously, and any
resemblance to actual persons, living or dead, business establishments,
events, or locales is entirely coincidental.

Paperback ISBN: 978-1-64108-026-2
Digital ISBN: 978-1-64080-558-3
Library of Congress Control Number: 2018961347
Paperback published April 2019
v. 1.0

Printed in the United States of America
∞
This paper meets the requirements of
ANSI/NISO Z39.48-1992 (Permanence of Paper).

LAQUETTE is an erotic, multicultural romance author of M/F and M/M love stories. Her writing style brings intellect to the drama. She often crafts emotionally epic, fantastical tales that are deeply pigmented by reality's paintbrush. Her novels are filled with a unique mixture of savvy, sarcastic, brazen, and unapologetically sexy characters who are confident in their right to appear on the page.

This bestselling Erotic Romance Author is the 2016 Author of the Year Golden Apple Award Winner, 2016 Write Touch Award Winner for Best Contemporary Midlength Novel, 2016 Swirl Awards 1st Place Winner in Romantic Suspense, and 2016 Aspen Gold Award Finalist in Erotic Romance. LaQuette—a native of Brooklyn, New York—spends her time catering to her three distinct personalities: Wife, Mother, and Educator.

At the age of sixteen, LaQuette read her first romance novel and realized the genre was missing something: people who looked and lived like her. As a result, her characters and settings are always designed to provide positive representations of people of color and various marginalized communities.

She loves hearing from readers and discussing the crazy characters that are running around in her head causing so much trouble. Contact her on her website, www.LaQuette.com, on Facebook at Facebook.com/LaQuetteTheAuthor, Twitter at @LaQuetteWrites, Amazon, Instagram at @la_quette, and via email at LaQuette@LaQuette.com.

Chapter One

"**TRAFFIC** detected ahead in 1.5 miles. Take suggested alternate route instead."

Camden Warren cringed at the automated voice coming from his GPS. "God," he groaned. "Even the disembodied robotic voice in my navigator thinks I need to be directed everywhere."

He begrudgingly made the necessary adjustments to his route, hoping nothing else deterred his journey home.

One hand on the steering wheel, the other rubbing the tension from his neck, Camden replayed the conversation—or more aptly termed, the civil disagreement—he and his father had engaged in. Two hours spent at his parents' "Downstate" home in Kings Point, Long Island, playing verbal tennis all to answer one question.

"When are you going to choose a suitable man to settle down with whose pedigree will be an asset to you on the campaign trail? I've presented you several suitable candidates over the last five years, Camden. You've tossed them all away. You will not ignore this opportunity I've cultivated with the senator's son."

Michael Warren, chief judge of the New York Court of Appeals, had one goal in mind: for his son, Camden, to blaze across the political arena. It wasn't a bad dream to have. If Camden were to be honest, the idea of holding office, and having the ability to change the government, was intoxicating. Enticing enough he'd followed every letter of his father's master plan to political nirvana. Everything except the need for a pretty spouse to smile nicely for the cameras.

"A 97 percent conviction rate. Executive assistant district attorney in less than ten years on the job. All of that, and I'm still not good enough to win an election if I don't have the right man by my side?"

Halfway through his trip, a blinking light on his dashboard illuminated the car. It was one of those safety features that screamed at you to take care of your vehicle when you'd otherwise ignore it.

A quick glance at the dash showed him it was the low-fuel alarm. His car was doubtful Camden could make it home at his current speed with only a quarter tank of gas in the car.

Camden slammed his hand against the steering wheel. "Apparently, everyone is questioning my judgment tonight."

He glanced down Conduit Avenue until he saw the familiar sign of a franchise gas station shining in the night. After turning the indicator on, he drove into the station and pulled up to a pump.

He leaned down, trying to spot any attendants who might be around, and prickled in annoyance when he saw the self-service sign. Not that he'd never pumped his own gas before, but after going ten rounds with his dad about settling down with a suitable husband, Camden just wanted to be done with this task as soon as possible.

Taking a deep breath to pull himself together, he turned the car off, exited, and walked to the pump controls. Pulling his credit card out of his wallet, he was about to swipe it when he saw the "Credit cards pay inside" message scrolling across the small screen.

"Shit! Can this get any worse?"

Camden shoved his card back in his pocket and made the trek across all eight pumps before he reached the little market he assumed the "inside" part of the message referred to.

He stepped inside, seeing an empty cashier's booth in the front of the store. He stood there, tapping his finger against the reinforced plastic cube where someone should've been sitting so he could get his gas and get the hell on the road.

When a young man with stringy brown hair came through a door marked Employees Only, he almost threw his credit card at the kid to get his attention.

"Fill it up on pump eight. Premium please."

"You got ID?"

Camden's jaw ticked with frustration. The kid was lucky that cube protected him from Camden's need to wring his scrawny little neck. He pulled his driver's license from his wallet and threw it into the drawer the boy had pushed open.

"You need a receipt?"

"No," he growled. "I need you to turn the pump on, so I can get my gas and go home."

Camden pinched the bridge of his nose and shook his head as he mentally chastised himself. He was being an asshole to this kid when his frustration lay solely at his father's feet, and that was unacceptable. Remorseful, and with a minor attitude adjustment, Camden dropped his hand to his side and stared at the attendant. "I'm sorry. It's been a rough night."

The kid shrugged his shoulders, not seeming at all concerned with Camden's impatience or his apology, and went about the business of scanning the card, having Camden sign for the purchase, and sliding the card back through the push-pull drawer for him to collect.

His card in his wallet, and hopefully a working gas pump waiting for him, Camden left the mini-mart and headed toward his car. He was halfway there when he realized the adolescent behind the window hadn't given him back his driver's license.

Camden turned on his heel and headed back. When his hand reached the door, he heard a loud sound that resembled a large vehicle backfiring. A quick glance over his shoulder revealed a strange spark near his muffler.

"What the fuck is that?"

He made one step toward the car as the spark happened again, and a loud boom filled the air. Camden stood disoriented and uncertain of what was occurring, when an unseen force pushed him through the air and back into the swinging doors of the mini-mart.

His surroundings were suddenly quiet and dark. Strangely, it was the silence that panicked him most. Why couldn't he hear anything? What was that loud boom before everything went so quiet? Since when was he able to fly?

There were a million questions in his mind he wanted to ask. But suddenly, the most pertinent impulse seemed to be his need to close his eyes and succumb to the darkness.

Chapter Two

ELIJAH Stephenson stood outside of the metal double doors of the seventy-fourth precinct. Half of him was ready to walk away while the other half nudged Elijah to open the doors and step inside.

Fourteen years of running in and out of this place and he'd never hesitated to enter its walls. This was Elijah's house, his home, and his brothers and sisters in blue lived inside. Yet standing there on the outside, disconnected like a severed limb, phantom memories of a career path lost to him haunted Elijah's soul.

Six months had passed since he'd last entered this building. Then, he was Sergeant Elijah Stephenson, badass vice detective who stared down the bottom feeders determined to bleed his Brooklyn community dry. He stomped on the pimps, drug dealers, and gun runners in East New York, and he'd taken pleasure in doing it. He was on a professional high until he was shot, beaten, and left for dead in an ambush.

Elijah took another breath, trying to squash the memories that threatened to creep through his subconscious and make it to the forefront of his mind.

He'd survived. That was the mantra he kept repeating whenever flashes of the attack returned. It was something his department therapist had taught him. No matter what happened in the past, he was still here in the present. He was still alive.

He was still alive, and things had changed.

He'd taken the lieutenant's exam before he was injured. His receipt of his passing test scores and a letter of intent regarding his promotion had helped pull him out of his slump and given him motivation to work on his injuries, both inside and out. Now, he stood in front of these doors, Lieutenant Stephenson, and as soon as he built up the nerve to open them, there would be a new, safer command waiting for him.

This new command was so much more than a new duty assignment. It represented a new life for Elijah. He'd work from an office. He'd work normal hours and have weekends off. He'd be able to sleep in his bed at night, even go out, and do something as routine as go on a date.

Damn, when was the last time you had a date, man?

He stood there trying to recall his last real date. He'd had hookups, but hooking up for a night wasn't the same thing as dating. He spent just enough time with those men to get his rocks off and move on to the next man, the next case, that came afterward. But the last date he remembered was with that asshole his friend Lindsey had set him up with five years ago.

Cocky and stuck on himself, the man was sexy as hell. He was clean-shaven and too pretty for Elijah to ignore, and against his better judgment, he'd let the date progress until they were back at Elijah's place, sweating up his damn sheets. The guy's arrogance notwithstanding, Elijah had never forgotten his touch or his taste. A fact that still pissed him off after all this time.

With not so much as a "See you later. Come lock your door," his date absconded while Elijah slept and had never contacted Elijah again.

He was pissed about it. In part because Elijah had always been that guy who snuck away, but also because the man had left his door unlocked. As a cop who knew what lurked outside in the streets, sleeping with an unlocked door was a game he didn't play.

Elijah carried the sting of that brush-off for as long as he took to realize the brunet cutie had done him a favor. The lifestyle he led as a vice cop would have allowed nothing more than a few sessions in his bed.

But it was over now. Elijah had paid his dues and sacrificed more than enough to the job. This new appointment meant Elijah was getting his life back. All he had to do was walk inside and claim it.

"You can do this, Stephenson. Just man up."

He pulled one door open and entered the concrete walls of the seventy-fourth. The familiar smell of industrial cleaner was the first thing to grab his attention. He coughed as the potent chemicals made the back of his throat tickle.

He shook his head. In the fourteen years he'd spent in and out of this building, Elijah never noticed how caustic the stench of that cleaner was.

Maybe it's not the cleaner. Maybe you're not up to this anymore.

Somewhat shaken by the thoughts zipping across his mind, he closed his eyes and reminded himself of what awaited him. Vice was behind him. He'd given his all and then some to the streets. Now, it was time for a different life. A more fulfilling one that didn't involve him getting shot at as a normal job occurrence.

When he made his way into the squadron, the bustling sounds customary to a busy police station stopped, and the open space filled with quiet. Elijah looked around the room and watched as his fellow officers focused their eyes on him.

The awkward pause made his heartbeat speed up and his brow dampen with a thin mist of sweat. The silence seemed endless until Elijah heard the distant sound of flesh slapping together in the distance. The sound grew, one officer after another joining in the applause until the sound of hand-clapping filled the room.

Elijah nodded, keeping his eyes focused on Captain Searlington's office, trying his best not to make eye contact with any of his fellow officers. He didn't want their praise. Didn't deserve it. Not when he'd lost the best part of himself in those streets during his attack. A cop with no nerve, was there anything more useless?

He plowed through the throng of officers, accepting their welcome-backs and cheerful slaps on the back as he kept moving toward his destination. As he reached the metal door with the acrylic window that read *Captain Searlington* on it, he tapped against the glass, then waited for the customary "Come in" before he entered.

When he opened the door, a tall woman with deep brown skin, an athletic build, and her dark brown hair pulled into a tight ponytail, stood up from her desk and walked around to greet him with her hand extended.

"Glad to have you back, Stephenson," she stated as she offered him her hand. "How are you feeling?"

"I'm fine." He gave her a brief smile as he answered and took the seat she offered him in front of her desk.

"I know what it's like getting injured in the field. I wouldn't blame you if you needed more time off. Lord knows you've got it banked."

She wasn't lying. Elijah had more sick time than he knew what to do with. So much so, he'd never had a lapse in paychecks while waiting for the city to take their slow-ass time to get his disability benefits together. His stockpile of sick and vacation time was just proof of how obsessed he was with his work.

Back then, he'd believed only bored people needed time off. Why would he need to get away from something he loved so much? Except for a mandatory week the department forced on him here or there, Elijah had never wanted to be away from his work for longer than it took for him to sleep, work out, and come back.

"So, you sure you're ready to get back to duty?"

There were slight lines pulling at Captain Searlington's brow as she waited for his answer. She was worried about him.

He dropped his gaze for just a moment, closing his eyes to gather his thoughts. According to his head and body docs, he was fit for duty. His captain no doubt had copies of those reports. She knew he was cleared to return, but looking into the warm brown eyes staring at him from across the desk, he understood what she was truly asking.

Are you sure you're ready for me to put a gun and a badge in your hand again?

"Captain. I'm good. Besides, it's either return to work or die from being smothered by my family."

"Ms. Evelyn's just concerned about her son. There's nothing wrong with that," she countered. "But if you're ready to get back, I'm glad to give you these."

She reached into a desk drawer and pulled out his Glock, its magazine, and his credentials. "Welcome back, Lieutenant Stephenson."

He took the weapon, inspected it, and then slid the magazine inside the well. He took a moment to secure it at his hip, and then he grabbed for his new badge and smiled.

Before the shooting, he hadn't cared about climbing up the ladder. Making detective allowed him to work in Vice, and earning his sergeant's rank meant he got to lead his teams and operations the way he chose in the field. The only reason he'd taken the test was to appease his father, a retired NYPD officer who wanted bragging rights about his first-born becoming a white shirt.

As always, his father was right. This new shield and rank were the only reason he still had a place in this building. After everything he'd been through, he wasn't sure he could handle being on the streets any longer.

"So, when do I officially take over my new command, Captain?"

She leaned back and tapped her fingers against her desk. "About that."

Elijah had known Heart Searlington for too long not to be concerned by that statement. Something wasn't right.

"What's up, Captain?"

"There was a situation last night."

Elijah repositioned himself in his chair, instinct telling him he needed to seek comfort. His superior was crossing her arms against her chest, so he figured things were about to get uncomfortable for him.

"Brass has delayed your transfer into Cybercrimes," she answered. "Instead, they want to put you on a protection detail for a high-profile target."

Elijah shook his head before he found his voice. "Captain? This wasn't what I agreed to when I came back. They promised me Cybercrimes. Brass can't take that from me."

She held up her hand to stop him. "Stephenson, we both know brass can do whatever the hell they want. You and I are only here to do what they tell us. This comes directly from the top cop, Elijah. Even I can't ignore it. You protect this guy for a few days. Then you'll get your command afterward."

"And what happens if I refuse?" His question lingered in the air for a moment. She sat straighter in her chair, pushing her shoulders back, painting the picture of authority in the room.

"If you refuse," she began, "then I'll be taking that new position and that shiny new lieutenant's badge. I told you, Stephenson, this is coming from on top. You've built a career on not being afraid of shit and taking on any foe. They want someone with that kind of heart to head this detail."

Elijah pulled his hand down his face and let a long breath escape his lips. He'd been cracking heads and making busts for years. It had never put him on anyone's radar before.

"What's happened? Why does brass want me on this instead of cybercrimes?"

"As I hear it, the DA asked for you by name. She said she trusted no one else to protect her number two but you. So, if you're blaming anyone for this, point a finger at her."

Elijah closed his eyes and shook his head. Lindsey Chavez, Brooklyn district attorney, Elijah's longtime friend, and the resident busybody in his life. He should have known his friend's hand was involved.

Captain Searlington picked up a file and slid it across her desk in his direction, pulling his focus back to their conversation. "Here's what you need to know. They're called The Path of Unity."

"The church group?" He'd seen advertisements for them on the train and on television. He couldn't say he knew much about them other than that half of Hollywood seemed connected with the group.

"They're a cult with a history of organized crime, Stephenson. If they were Sicilian or Russian, we'd call them the Mob. They're passing themselves off as a church. We've known of their criminal activity for years, but we couldn't build a solid case against them. A few months ago, we found a way into the organization and discovered enough info to indict the top man, Lee Edwards, and two of his cronies. The DA's office could bring charges and make them stick. They're in the middle of a trial right now. Edwards is out on bail, but if the prosecutors do their job, his days of freedom are numbered."

"So, what's the problem?" Elijah knew there was more. There was always more when dealing with crazy situations like this one.

"They tried to take out the prosecutor assigned to the case," Captain Searlington answered. "They put a bomb under his car. The only reason he survived was that he stopped for gas. Getting out of the car to go pay the attendant saved his life."

"Shit," he replied. "A bomb? They weren't playing, huh?"

The captain shook her head as she stood up from her desk and walked around to the front.

"This ADA they tried to get at wasn't just your run-of-the-mill prosecutor. He's the executive assistant district attorney. His father is the chief judge in the New York Court of Appeals."

"Captain, this sounds like it's gonna be fucked on all sides. I didn't sign on for this."

She crossed her arms over her chest again, letting him know she was pulling rank on him in just that simple move.

"Doesn't matter," she answered. "It's your detail, or it's your career. If you want that cushy job, you're gonna have to protect this executive ADA."

She leaned over the desk and pushed a button on her phone. "Send him in," she said before returning her attention to Elijah. "I know it's fucked-up, Stephenson. But it's the job."

It was a job that seemed to have him by the balls whether or not he wanted to admit it. He picked the file up off the desk and flipped through its pages. If he would put his neck on the line for some legal VIP, the least he could do was know what he was up against.

"It's about time. You've kept me in the bowels of this building, locked up like I'm a criminal. In case you've forgotten, it was my car someone blew up last night."

Elijah's ears tingled at the sound of that voice. There was something about its tone that his mind latched on to. Confident, and not just the normal "I've got a big set of balls" bluster. No, there was the eerie sound of expectation coloring the tone of his words. As if he knew he was important enough to listen to.

Elijah's body tensed as he remembered the last time he'd heard that voice. Goose bumps raised the hairs on his arms, making his skin prickle with either anticipation, anxiety, or anger. The truth was his heart was beating so fast as he processed the familiar voice, he couldn't say exactly which was the case.

"It can't be. No, it cannot be," he whispered to himself as that voice continued to carry on behind Elijah.

"Mr. Warren, I've just finished briefing my lieutenant on your case. He's a decorated officer, and he will keep you safe until we lock the crazies away," Searlington said.

Elijah rolled his eyes and shook his head as he heard the name Warren cross Captain Searlington's lips. Tapping his foot on the floor as he tried to ignore the tightness building in his chest, Elijah refused to believe this could happen to him.

He'd left his house ready to begin a new chapter in his life, a safer, more relaxed phase. Instead of giving him the pencil-pushing gig brass had promised, they slapped him straight in the middle of hell.

"So where is this great detective? I can't sit around in your precinct all day, Captain Searlington. I've got a trial to prepare for."

Elijah replaced the file on his captain's desk and stood up. He turned and found the owner of the pushy voice. Even before he'd laid eyes on him, Elijah's mind had conjured up the five-year-old image in his head. Jet-black hair, blue eyes, and lips soft as butter. A brief flash of Elijah running his tongue across that mouth, tasting every inch, flitted across his mind.

The memory was appealing at first. Then, the uncomfortable aftermath popped into Elijah's head and pushed the memory to the back of his mind where it belonged.

"I'm right here, Camden," Elijah said. "Or has it been that long you no longer recognize me?"

Chapter Three

CAMDEN turned around at the call of his name. His gaze followed the familiar sound until he was staring into eyes he hadn't seen for five years.

Still tall, with long locs still hanging just below his shoulders, and a trimmed goatee. Skin still the same color as smooth, tanned oak. Camden's eyes continued to travel down a broad chest and shoulders that made his fingers itch to caress them. Arms still wide with carved muscle, and a lean waist that tapered down into a thin vee made Camden swallow to push the dry knot blocking his airway free.

He forced his eyes closed as his gaze fell on the metal belt buckle sitting at the bottom of this walking memory's waist. If he continued his perusal, if he kept remembering the fire that burned through him with every touch and taste of his tormentor's body parts, this encounter was liable to turn into something very different from a police matter.

"Elijah?"

Camden shook his head, uncertain why he'd said the man's name as if it were a question. This was Elijah Stephenson. Hard, beautiful, and so sexy he made Camden's mouth water.

"You remember my name? I'm impressed," Elijah added.

Remember? Camden laughed at that. Who in the hell could forget a real-life walking sex dream? If big, muscular men with an imposing presence were your cup of tea, Elijah Stephenson was a person you wouldn't soon forget.

Camden was no slouch. His bulk remained tight with a personalized fitness plan that kept his muscle shirts filled and his jeans fitted. But Elijah didn't need a gym plan or a personal trainer. His physique and power came from things like running down criminals on the street and lifting cinder blocks or some such real-world thing Camden would never engage in. He didn't care to get his own hands soiled, but a man who liked to play in the grit of life was always Camden's weakness.

Camden blinked his eyes again, flipped the switch in his head that turned on his prosecutor's facade. Hands on his waist, shoulders pushed back, and eyes narrowed at his target. Camden stepped toward Elijah, refusing to let his memories or the delicious sight Elijah made shake his fortitude.

"Why are you here, Elijah? How are you involved with my case?"

"I'm your assigned babysitter, Counselor."

Camden caught the faint hint of amusement in Elijah's voice, and his mood soured. To keep his calm, he dismissed Elijah with a cold glare and turned to the captain at his side. "Not a possibility. Get someone else," he demanded.

"Mr. Warren," Captain Searlington began. If the deep breath she'd taken just before she said his name was any sign, she wasn't all that thrilled with Camden now.

Camden sighed and pressed his fingers firmly against his temple. If he were the man his father raised him to be, he'd be throwing his weight around right now, making demands of everyone in the room. But after how poorly Camden behaved five years ago, treating Elijah like a discarded one-off, he found it difficult to muster up his practiced asshole tendencies.

"Mr. Warren, Lieutenant Stephenson has an impressive career record. He is the best at what he does."

Camden ran a frantic hand through his raven locks. "And what does Lieutenant Stephenson do?"

"He has a nose for sniffing out the bad guys. He's the best tactical mind I've seen in our house in a long time. He also has a protective streak for simpletons who find themselves in situations they can't get out of. And when he's called on to protect someone who can't defend themselves, he locks like a Pit and doesn't let go until either he or the threat is destroyed."

Camden's shoulders rose with every breath he drew in through his flared nostrils. Did she call him a simpleton? Did she reprimand him without so much as raising her voice?

"So," Captain Searlington continued, "are there other officers I can assign this case? Yes. But if you want to live through this experience, I'd suggest Lieutenant Stephenson is the man for the job."

The lady captain sauntered back to her desk, otherwise unbothered by the exchange they'd just had.

"Lieutenant Stephenson," she continued, "the office next to Lieutenant Smyth's is now yours." She opened a desk drawer and plucked out a set of keys, tossing them in the air to Elijah. "You can move in now. Take the ADA there and get started on his case. As of now, you're attached at the hip. Are we clear, Lieutenant?"

Camden watched in quiet awe as Elijah nodded his head, agreeing to the calm command given by his superior. Even though this woman might be Elijah's boss, she wasn't Camden's. He wasn't about to let her decide how to keep him safe while she acted as if Camden wasn't even present in the room.

"Your cop might agree to that, Captain. But I don't. I will not allow this man to invade my privacy."

The woman sat down in her chair and made a slow point of removing her gun from her hip, then setting it on her desk as she gave the weapon a gentle caress. The move was simple, but it drew his attention and kept Camden's eyes on her. A fact he was certain was the point of her actions.

"Mr. Warren, it's either your privacy or your funeral. Which do you prefer?"

Camden swallowed hard as a chill spilled down his spine. After last night's events, choosing between the two alternatives wasn't difficult at all.

"Which way to your office, Lieutenant Stephenson?"

ELIJAH sat back in his new, mostly empty office, trying to get his head right. Unfortunately, Camden Warren's presence was an unavoidable distraction he couldn't ignore.

"If this is your new office, I'd hate to see what the old one looked like," Camden commented while he stood in the center of the small room and turned in a slow circle to survey the place.

"The office is new to me, as in it came with my new rank and command," Elijah responded.

"You've been promoted? I always knew you'd make something of yourself. What kind of unit are you being assigned to?"

Did this motherfucker just low-key insult me? Elijah threw the file Captain Searlington had given him onto the empty desk and leaned back in his chair. "Listen. There's no need for the small talk. I'm here to do a job, and you're here because someone is trying to kill you. If you haven't been worried about my life enough to call over the last five years, my new promotion shouldn't be of any concern to you now."

Elijah returned his focus to the file as he heard Camden take the few steps to the seat in front of Elijah's desk.

"Bitter much, Detective?"

Elijah pulled his nose from the papers in front of him and lifted a skeptical brow.

"Bitter? To be bitter, I'd have to care. We fucked. It was fun, but that's all it was. I had no illusions it would be otherwise. The dick was good."

A flash of memory zipped across Elijah's mind, reminding him just how good Camden had been. Good didn't accurately describe the way the lawyer made Elijah's entire body burn with need that night.

It didn't matter, though. Elijah for damn sure wasn't about to share that bit of info and contribute to Camden's already inflated ego. Nope, he'd just swallow the appreciation he had for Camden's stroke game and keep it to himself.

"But just so you know," Elijah continued, "I don't make a habit of laying with bad fucks. You weren't special. It didn't mean shit then, and it has no bearing on how I do my job five years later. Get over yourself, and let's get to work on your case."

Camden's Adam's apple bobbed as the man swallowed.

He shoots. He scores.

The minor action told Elijah he'd stuck a pin in Camden's "I'm better than everybody else" perspective of himself. With that settled, maybe they'd get some work done since their focus was off how sexy Camden was then—and now, if Elijah was to be honest.

"Executive ADA Warren," Elijah stated with his matter-of-fact cop tone in play, "why does the Path of Unity want you dead?"

notepad in front of him than to Camden, he readjusted his position in the chair, hoping to distract himself from the beautiful specimen of man sitting before him.

"So, if they've killed witnesses before, why escalate their crimes by killing an ADA? Why not just kill off another witness?"

"Because I'm the only person who knows where she is," Camden answered. "This witness has been through enough at the hands of these people. I didn't want her to sacrifice anything more for them."

"But I'm sure the defense knows who she is and what she has to say. Didn't you have to turn over that info in discovery?"

Camden shook his head. This wasn't your typical case, and he'd had to commit some serious legal acrobatics to get things this far. The Path was smart, and lethal. They had no issues with doing whatever was necessary to win. Whether it was a witness or an officer of the court, they'd annihilate any threat to them.

"No. I petitioned the court for an ex parte meeting. After citing the suspicious deaths of the previous witnesses, the judge agreed that I could hide this witness and deliver her to the court for her testimony," Camden answered as he thought back to his conversation with the judge. Judge Simmons was a by-the-book judge. It would take an act of God to get her to do anything unorthodox in her courtroom. He'd had to put together a compelling argument comprising circumstantial evidence and witness affidavits to get her to even consider allowing him to keep the witness stashed from the defense until testimony. "She'll grant a brief continuance after the witness's testimony if the defense so desires, but Judge Simmons isn't announcing the witness's identity to anyone until she's called to testify in court."

"So, if they can't kill or scare the witness, they'll move on to the prosecutor? That's a ballsy strategy," Elijah commented as he dropped his pen on the writing pad and leaned back in his chair.

"These people have proven to be ruthless. They'll kill whomever they need to remain free." That knowledge made Camden shiver. In doing his job to protect the public, he'd placed himself right in the sights of a murderous foe.

"Cam," Elijah called to him, his voice colored with compassion and concern. "I know last night couldn't have been easy. I can't say I'm happy about being assigned to this case. But I'll do what I have to keep you safe."

The intensity in Elijah's eyes calmed the fear Camden had been struggling with since he'd watched his car explode last night. He'd treated this man poorly, even if it had been for Elijah's own good, and now, here Elijah sat offering Camden comfort during the most traumatic experience of Camden's life. Somehow that knowledge hollowed him out, filling the important parts of him with emptiness and shame. Even when he tried to do the right thing, he still screwed it up.

Camden shook his head, trying to crawl out of the weird space his thoughts were taking him to and focused on the issue at present. "So, what's your plan, Elijah?"

"Well, you're hiding the witness. So, I will hide you."

"Where are you going to hide me?"

Elijah leaned forward, placing his elbows on the desk and bending his luscious lips into an inviting smile. "That, Counselor, is on a need-to-know basis, and you don't need to know."

ELIJAH unlocked the door and took a deep, calming breath when he stepped inside the uninhabited Westchester home. Even though he wasn't here under pleasurable circumstances, just being inside these walls had a way of healing his restless soul. He stepped aside, holding the door open for Camden, waiting for the man to enter. Once he was inside, Elijah headed toward the living room and motioned for Camden to follow him.

"This is nice," Camden uttered as he stepped in a slow circle, looking around the room. "NYPD's safehouses are nicer than I thought they'd be. I was imagining some seedy hotel scene from *Law and Order*."

"It's not NYPD's. It's mine."

Camden stopped turning long enough to make eye contact with Elijah. "This is yours? Really?"

Elijah narrowed his eyes, trying hard not to let Camden get under his skin. It seemed the man's arrogance seeped through all the time. "What, surprised a dumb cop could buy something like this?"

Elijah waved his hand across the expanse of the spacious room. It was a four-thousand-square-foot colonial sitting on three-quarters of an acre of land. Elijah had scrimped and saved for years, taking all of that hazard pay and overtime and putting it toward a sizable down payment for this house. It was the thing he was most proud of, and to have this man insult Elijah in it rubbed him the wrong way.

"No." Camden raised his hands palm-side up in surrender. "That wasn't what I was saying at all, Elijah." Camden dropped his eyes. For someone as arrogant as him, Elijah was certain it was as close to an act of contrition as he'd get. "I was just surprised you'd bring me to your place. Isn't this a breach of protocol or something?"

"Normally it would be. But my captain wants you somewhere that no one else can trace you to. That eliminates any place connected to NYPD or the DA's office. And since you and I have no documented history together, this is probably the last place anyone would look for you."

Camden nodded, still looking everywhere but at Elijah as he spoke. "I guess it just feels a little weird being back in a place of yours again. Especially in this situation."

"You mean after you fucked and ran the last time?" The slight hint of rose coloring beneath Camden's creamy skin let Elijah know his comment had hit its mark. "No one knows about this place. The only people who ever come here are my parents and sibling. The only address I have on file is my apartment in Brooklyn. If anyone goes snooping, they shouldn't be able to connect you or me to this place. It's the perfect hideout."

"So, you're not expecting any company, then?" Camden's question made Elijah chuckle and shake his head. The balls on this guy were unbelievable.

"You couldn't possibly be asking me if I'm expecting a date to arrive?" Elijah walked to where Camden was standing. They were matched in height, but Elijah had more bulk to his muscular frame than the lithe runner's build Camden possessed. He leaned in, crowding Camden enough that the man looked poised to take a step back. "Could you?"

Camden shook his head and cleared his throat. "No, I just wanted to make sure we were safe here. That's all."

"We're safe," Elijah replied, knowing it was only a half truth. Elijah doubted anyone looking for Camden

would ever find him here. NYPD had smuggled him
into the precinct from the hospital after the explosion
and smuggled him out of the precinct through an
underground parking lot into Elijah's tinted SUV. No,
unless these cult members could mind read, no one
would know where Elijah had stashed him.

But the way Elijah's blood simmered as he stood this
close to Camden, breathing in the acrid scent of medicinal
soap wafting off his skin, Elijah didn't think safe was
the right word to describe their current status. Slightly
intoxicated by the desire Elijah knew he shouldn't have
for a man he shouldn't want, Elijah paused a second
to let his gaze slide up and down Camden's lean body.
A moment was all it took to remember how glorious
Camden was in nothing but his bare skin, and for Elijah
to recognize the real threat Camden was. They might
have been safe from Camden's enemies, but being safe
from each other was another matter altogether.

"Now." Elijah uttered the single word through
a dry mouth, taking a moment to swallow before he
spoke again. "Let's go upstairs so I can show you where
you'll be sleeping."

Elijah turned around, heading for the steps, forcing
himself not to look back at the tempting sight of a wide-
eyed Camden standing in the middle of his living room.
Instead he kept putting one foot in front of the other,
reminding himself that fucking around with Camden,
no matter how good he knew it would feel, was a bad
idea. The way his life was set up, Elijah couldn't afford
any wrong moves right now.

Once Camden was settled in the guest room, Elijah
fell across his bed. He would've stayed there for the
rest of the day, but knew he had to place a call first.
Elijah turned over and fished around for the disposable

cell phone in his pocket, connected the call and waited for his captain to pick up on the other end.

"Everything all right?"

"Yeah, we arrived a few moments ago. He's settling in."

There was a brief pause before she continued. Not long enough to be awkward, but definitely long enough to make the hairs on his arms stand up. "I'm glad you called. I was actually about to dial you. There's been a development."

Elijah sat up on the bed, pinned the phone between his ear and his shoulder, and started putting his sneakers back on. "What happened?"

"We've got intel. Our informant on the inside says Lee is dispatching men to look for Camden. To find out if he's really dead."

Elijah stood up and gave his neck a good roll. They'd blown the man's car up. Would it be too much for them to believe they'd won and let shit go?

"Is that the line we're feeding the press, that he's dead?"

"We're using the excuse of charred wreckage and remains and a busy forensics lab to keep Camden's identity concealed. On its face, our story's holding. But Lee Edwards isn't stupid. If he was, we'd have built a solid case against him a long time ago."

Elijah stepped inside of his closet in search of his to-go bag. "Maybe we should set up another location." He closed his hand around the small duffel bag's handle and opened it for a quick perusal.

"No. For all we know this could be a plan to draw him out. Don't move until I tell you to or the threat level has increased."

Elijah closed the bag and moved it to the side of his dresser just in case he needed to move quickly later. For now, Captain Searlington was right. Staying put was the safest bet. "I'll await further instructions."

Chapter Five

CAMDEN woke from his nap with a dull ache behind his eyes. He was exhausted. But despite the bone-deep fatigue, he couldn't seem to sleep any longer. It was probably normal for people who'd survived an attempt on their life to have a bout of insomnia or two. But Camden wasn't certain his current sleeplessness was because of the trauma or the knowledge that Elijah Stephenson, and all his sexiness, was somewhere roaming this house.

Why did it have to be him?

Camden could still remember the night of their blind date. Lindsey had worked for the better part of six months trying to get the two of them together. She'd sung Elijah's praises, making him sound like the most delicious piece of man meat to ever walk, until Camden had agreed to a solitary date. The two men texted back and forth for a week before agreeing on a casual dinner at a local eatery near Camden's office.

Camden had walked into the restaurant, dressed in a fitted long-sleeved muscle shirt and designer jeans he knew displayed every bit of the carved lean muscle he and his trainer worked so hard on. Even through the throng of the Saturday night crowd, based on Lindsey's description, Camden could spot Elijah easily. Beautiful brown skin with reddish undertones, neatly twisted dark brown locs that swept his shoulders, a broad build of hard muscle, and an ass that warranted worship. And she'd been right. Elijah was beautiful, built to perfection with thick muscular legs that made him look edible in his jeans. But when the man took notice of Camden at the door and offered him a warm, bright smile, the part of Camden that kept him distanced from most people in the world, including the ones he shared blood with, begged him to let Elijah play for more than a night.

Camden had known then that Elijah was dangerous. Yes, there was a certain fearlessness about his aura, one that many cops in Camden's experience possessed. It was the bravado, the attitude that warned others to tread with caution when in their presence. Camden should've listened to the warning bells. Maybe if he had, he wouldn't have spent his brief rest tossing and turning, wondering if Elijah slept in his boxer briefs, or in the nude, the way Camden had left him five years earlier.

Camden groaned as both delightful images popped up in his mind. Too tired to jerk off and too annoyed to stay in bed, Camden rolled on his side, then swung his legs out of the bed. He sat for a moment, taking a deep breath in to clear his head when the smell of something inviting filled the air.

He made his way to the bathroom down the hall and caught a glimpse of himself in the mirror. With none of the high-end salon products his own bathroom vanity would be littered with, his untamed jet-black waves hung freely over his brow. He wet his hands and ran them through his strands to provide some sort of control but gave up when his fussing only seemed to make his hair unrulier.

His stomach grumbled, and his need to preen momentarily forgotten, he washed his face, brushed his teeth, and threw on a pair of sweatpants and a T-shirt, both borrowed from Elijah. Camden was on his way out of the room and down the stairs, when the sound of music caught his attention. He followed the rhythmic beats of what sounded like an up-tempo mix of R&B, jazz, and hip hop to the kitchen. Camden's breath caught in his throat when his eyes lasered in on Elijah, his back to the kitchen entrance as he stood at the stove, mixing something on the stovetop, moving his body to the beat of the music.

From the bopping of his head, down to his swaying hips, Elijah's movements caressed the beat. His swaying body matched the peaks, valleys, and lulls of the music.

It was intoxicating.

Not just the sensual power of his movements— although that was enough to make his mouth dry with want. No, there was something more, something essential, carnal even, about the way Elijah moved. It was so much more than just a man dancing at his stove while he cooked. It was freedom.

A shiver ran down Camden's spine as recognition took hold. This wasn't the first time he'd recognized this freedom. It wasn't the first time this man's power had drawn him in, overwhelming his senses.

This freedom, which he'd only had the chance to sample for a few hours into the night, had forced Camden to stay away from Elijah. The one night they'd shared had been enough to tell Camden that Elijah, and the freedom woven into the fabric of his being, would never fit into Camden's world.

"You gonna stand there and watch me dance all night, or help set the table?"

The deep rumble of Elijah's voice was the perfect excuse Camden needed to loosen the grip a five-year-old memory had on him. He blinked a few times, waiting for his mind to slip back into the confident persona he was so used to portraying. When the uncertainty of Elijah's effect on him faded away, he fell into character. With a tilt of his lip into his signature cocksure smile, Camden was back.

Camden leaned against the doorjamb, angled his head, and smiled wider as he took in another healthy eyeful of the still-dancing lieutenant. "I don't know," Camden huffed. "The view from here is so perfect, moving would just spoil it." When Elijah ignored him, Camden stepped inside the kitchen, spreading his palms wide on the island that stood between them. "How'd you know I was standing there, anyway? Your cop sense tingled?"

Elijah shut off the stovetop and turned around with a steaming hot pan in his hand. He laid it atop a heat protectant mat on the counter before lifting his eyes to meet Camden's.

"Yeah, it was my cop sense." His face straight with a lifted brow, he pointed behind him. "Or, you know, it could've been the reflective surface of the stovetop exhaust."

Camden laughed, shaking his head as Elijah went about pulling plates and cutlery from hidden places in the modern kitchen and filling the dishes with food.

"Smells good in here," Camden hummed. "Like breakfast." He gave a passing look to the bacon, eggs, and biscuits Elijah placed in front of him and whispered to himself, "Greasy breakfast, it appears."

"What was that?"

Camden shook his head. "Oh nothing."

Elijah shrugged. "When I left here today, my intention was to stay at my apartment in Brooklyn. I didn't have a chance to make a grocery run, so it's either breakfast for dinner, or nothing."

Camden held up a hand. "Breakfast for dinner sounds divine."

"It's my mom's biscuit recipe taken up a notch with my dad's sweet and spicy jelly recipe. Some bacon and eggs added to it will set it off just right. I promise you're gonna love it." As if to demonstrate that fact, he quickly fixed a plate for himself and dug into it.

Elijah smiled. There was pride there as he ate. Camden was certain it had more to do with Elijah's parents than actual biscuits and jelly, and that knowledge made his heart tug a bit with sadness. He shook his head, not wishing to focus on the negative, so he zeroed in on Elijah's smile.

"Has your dad retired yet?"

Elijah's eyes squinted, and then a spark of recognition took hold. Had their one night together been so forgettable that Elijah hadn't remembered telling Camden he'd joined the force to follow in his dad's footsteps?

Just because you remember everything doesn't mean he does, Camden.

If Elijah remembered nothing from that night, Camden knew it was no one's fault but his own. He'd let fear pull him away from the most engaging man he'd ever met, and he could only blame himself. Well, himself, and the well-oiled machine that was his father's plan for his future.

"Yeah," Elijah answered as he met Camden's gaze, "about two years ago. Now, he spends most of his days watching the Cooking Channel, and his nights making wonderful meals for my mom. They're both in heaven. His retirement seems to agree with them both. And your dad?"

Camden shook his head as a derisive chuckle shook his shoulders. "They'll pluck the gavel from his cold, dead hand before Chief Judge Warren retires from the New York Court of Appeals."

"I know having a dad with an impressive record in the department was difficult for me," Elijah hedged. "I can't imagine what it must be like for you knowing your dad was—is—the head honcho in the highest court in the state."

Smothering.

That was the only way Camden could describe it. On paper, it made for an amazing read. But to live that existence, always needing to be perfect for fear of besmirching the family name and legacy—yeah, no fun at all.

"I guess you don't think about it when you know no other way to be," Camden huffed as if balancing those heavy scales all his life hadn't been a living hell. The song playing cued a transition, and Camden allowed it to pull him away from the heavy conversation they'd found themselves in.

"I love this song," Camden spoke, not waiting to see if Elijah would acknowledge his subject change. "'Left & Right' was a club favorite." Camden bopped his head to D'Angelo's deep bass rhythms. "There are a few hits on the *Voodoo* album, but I'll always favor *Brown Sugar*."

Elijah lifted his head, his eyes narrowing into slits as he focused on Camden. "You would've been what, twelve or thirteen when *Brown Sugar* was popular, fifteen or sixteen when the *Voodoo* album dropped? What the hell would you have known about a neosoul king like D'Angelo at that point?"

"We're the same age, Elijah," Camden huffed, snatching a piece of crispy bacon from his plate. "Why is it so crazy I would've known about D'Angelo and not crazy you would?"

"Because I didn't grow up in one of those soulless boarding schools I'm assuming Mommy and Daddy sent you to. No way your headmaster would've allowed you to pollute your precious mind with music like that."

"I don't think I like your presumptions," Camden responded, fighting to keep his own laughter at bay. He had attended boarding school throughout his formative years and then went away to an Ivy League institution to which his parents wrote large checks for him to attend.

"But am I wrong?"

Camden held in the laughter for as long as he could until it bubbled up from his chest and spilled past his lips. "No, you're not wrong. There wasn't any neosoul there. But when you have your own credit card, you can buy whatever CDs you like and play them on your portable CD player." He savored the smoky flavor of the bacon. Better to enjoy it now. When he went back to his regularly scheduled life, bacon and biscuits would be traded for fruit and nondairy yogurt. "I was listening to *Brown Sugar* in my dorm room at thirteen. By the *Voodoo* album's release, I had my first fake ID, and was dancing to 'Left & Right' in Manhattan clubs."

Camden closed his eyes and thought back to the simplicity of those times. His father's plan for his life had been so far off at that point, it didn't seem to strangle every breath of freedom Camden ached to steal away for himself.

"Between the music, the clubs, the superb selection of alcohol, and the cannabis—honestly, some of the best marijuana ever grown—yes, boarding school and college, those were the days."

Elijah placed his palms flat against the countertop and braced himself. "You do realize I'm a cop, right? You admitted to all types of felonious behavior in that whimsical skip down memory lane you were just taking."

Camden shrugged his shoulders. "And you do realize I'm one of the best trial attorneys on the circuit? I'm certain I could get any charge you lobbed at me set aside."

Elijah waved a dismissive hand and headed for the refrigerator, returning with a container of half-and-half before he pulled a carafe of coffee from his coffee maker. "Your arrogance will get you in serious trouble one of these days, Counselor." He filled a cup with the steaming liquid and slid it across to Camden, keeping his gaze fixed, making it impossible for Camden to escape if he wanted to. "If it hasn't already."

Again, the lieutenant's perception was spot-on. Camden's arrogance was as much a part of who he was as the ink-black color of his hair. His father had spent years conditioning Camden to the idea that entitlement was something to expect when your family's financial and societal legacies rivaled the Rockefellers.

Camden had never considered the consequences of doing his job. It was all a game of checking off wins as his conviction rate skyrocketed above his counterparts' in the DA's office. He'd never thought his desire to take on the big cases to amass professional acclaim would put a target on his back. When you believed you were untouchable, such things didn't cross your mind.

"Hey," Elijah called to Camden, pulling him out of his musings. "You all right?"

"I'm fine," Camden lied. He shoved a forkful of food into his mouth and chewed to keep himself from telling Elijah the truth: he was scared, and it was a foreign concept to him. "Just hoping you have some soy milk in the fridge for my coffee."

Elijah lifted a skeptical brow, his expression revealing his disbelief in Camden's statement. This ability to read Camden was proving to be inconvenient if not annoying.

"So, have you figured out how to stop the Path? You use that super cop sense to bust the case wide-open?"

Elijah shook his head as he finished his food, then rinsed his plate before putting it in the dishwasher. "Nope."

Camden couldn't tell if the straight face and matter-of-fact tone was an act or not. He'd only known the man for a night. He hadn't had the chance to learn the subtleties of his displays of humor.

"Are you at least trying?" Camden asked with expectation. There was someone after him; neither of them could afford to forget that.

"No," Elijah answered. "I'm not trying to stop the Path, Camden. It's not my job."

Camden crossed his arms against his chest and stared in disbelief. "Not your job?" he repeated with as much indignation as one could muster when you heard the most ridiculous statement made over the kitchen counter.

"Camden," Elijah continued, "I'm here to keep you safe."

A tingle spread through Camden's system as Elijah punctuated the word "safe" with a brief touch to Camden's hand.

"My captain has an investigative team trying to figure out how to finish the Path for good. My job is to keep you hidden and alive until it's time to get you back to the city for your big day in court. Until then, kick back and relax a few days."

When Camden's entire body tensed at the idea of relaxing in their current situation, Elijah gave his hand a reassuring squeeze. "I promise, Camden, nothing will happen out here."

It was such a small gesture, Elijah holding his hand to comfort him. But in the midst of the shitstorm he was now trying to bluff his way through, Camden hung on to the small sliver of hope Elijah was attempting to give him, while simultaneously trying to deny the sizzle of electricity that singed his skin. He took a slow breath as he wondered which was more dangerous: the threat on his life, or the attraction he held for the man tasked with protecting him.

Chapter Six

"I PROMISE, Camden, nothing will happen out here."

Elijah watched Camden with a careful eye, noticing the quiet signs of stress the man unknowingly exhibited. Camden's usual tanned complexion seemed much fairer. The sharp line of his jaw ticked from the rigid set of muscles holding it in place. There were worry lines etched into his forehead. Add in the nervous way he kept repeating Elijah's answers, the anxiety causing a mild lilt at the end of each sentence, turning it into a question, and Elijah had all he needed to recognize Camden was in distress.

When Elijah had met Camden, his confidence and charm had been the most attractive thing about him. He was charismatic and so certain of himself that he grabbed Elijah's attention. Yes, Camden was a beautiful specimen of a man. He was tall, built with carved, tanned, lean muscles that made Elijah's mouth water, and his fingers itched to touch every inch of Camden's skin. With that lethal combination, there was no way Elijah could've ignored how attractive Camden was.

It was the depth of intelligence and confidence in Camden's eyes, however, that kept Elijah's attention that night. Not the tight body or perfect smile.

Elijah had never been one to fall into the blue-eyed craze. In part because he'd never been with a man long enough to care about what his eye color was, but mostly because other than available and ready to fuck with no strings, Elijah didn't much care about the characteristics of the men who shared his bed. Camden was different for reasons Elijah couldn't explain then or now. Maybe it was the dark hair/blue eyes combo that pulled Elijah in. Or, perhaps, the way those bright eyes shone with mischief when Camden laughed. Whatever it was, within ten minutes of meeting Camden, Elijah was already getting excited about spending quality time with the handsome lawyer.

Now, it was those same eyes that helped Elijah see through Camden's bluster. Yeah, on any average day, Camden's confidence probably choked the air out of a room, but at this moment, fear billowed off of him in unmistakable waves. Camden wasn't just anxious; he was afraid. Somehow, that seemed wrong.

Camden had lost that fire that intoxicated Elijah upon their meeting, and witnessing that made his skin tight and uncomfortable, like it was missing some essential vitamin to keep it soothed and supple. Bizarre, because it was so opposite from who Camden was. But it was also strange because Elijah had firsthand experience on how devastating it was to lose that kind of confidence in yourself.

When Elijah was attacked, it was the first time he remembered ever being afraid. The first time he'd ever been concerned that he wasn't enough to get the job done. That doubt that formed while he was being beaten and bloodied was far worse than any of the resulting physical injuries he'd sustained. He'd lost his belief in himself during that assault. But somehow, observing the same thing happening in Camden's eyes made Elijah's chest ache in ways it hadn't when he'd experienced the same bottomless hell.

Sympathizing with Camden's loss, Elijah tightened his hold on Camden's hand, hoping his actions could convey what his words couldn't.

I've been there. I know how this hurts.

The vibrating phone in Elijah's pocket broke the spell. He cleared his throat, trying to dislodge the lump of emotion sitting in his airway before he answered.

"'Sup."

"It's Searlington," his captain answered. "You and your new roomie kill each other yet?"

Elijah ran his hand over the under braid taming his locs and laughed. "No, not yet anyway," he replied as he stole a quick glance at Camden. He wondered what it would take to remove the worry from his now-serious face. They seemed, for the moment, to be on the same page. How long this unexpected reprieve would last was beyond him, considering how easy it was for Camden to get on his nerves.

"I just got off the phone with your friend, the DA," Captain Searlington commented, instantly knotting Elijah's stomach into a ball of nerves. What had Lindsey done now? "You and Mr. Warren were like a match to gasoline in my office. I knew something was up, so I took your friend out for drinks to get her to spill her guts. E. Why didn't you tell me you had that kind of history with this dude? She didn't give me all the specifics, but she said the two of you had a thing until Camden fucked it up."

Elijah rolled his eyes and vowed to strangle Lindsey and her loose-ass lips when they met again. He saw enough pity in the eyes of his fellow officers and superiors after his injury. He didn't need his captain—the person who'd stayed with him, holding his hand until his family had arrived at the hospital—feeling sorry for him because of a one-night stand gone wrong.

"That was a long time ago," he answered, trying to keep his side of the conversation light for Camden's sake. "Believe me. It's not as deep as she makes it out to be. I think her job makes her put a dramatic spin on everything." Elijah looked into Camden's eyes, still tethered to the pull their depths had on him. "It was no big deal. It didn't mean a thing. It won't affect me doing my job."

His chest tightened as he spoke those words. He'd intended them to be resolute, to reassure Captain Searlington she had nothing to worry about. But even he could detect something was off as he spoke. Something made even Elijah doubt that this messy situation was anything but in his control.

He gave himself a mental shake. It didn't matter what had occurred in their past. Elijah would do what he was assigned to. Was he attracted to Camden? Would he rather not be on this case at all? The obvious answer was yes to both those questions. But the way Camden had discarded him all but ensured there would never be anything beyond this case between them. Even if Elijah wanted to act on this thing that pulled at him whenever he was in Camden's presence, he couldn't. Camden didn't want him.

"Nonetheless, I'm sorry, Elijah," Captain Searlington answered. "Now that I know the deal, if you want me to, I'll go to brass, see if I can get you pulled from this without it blowing back on you."

Elijah couldn't tell if it was relief or fear that washed over him. He closed his eyes, pinching the bridge of his nose as he contemplated his freedom. He was ready to give her the yes she was waiting for, but then he caught sight of Camden, still watching him, still weighed down with worry.

Elijah was a tactician. Except for that last sting where he'd moved without having all the information needed, Elijah had always followed the smart play. Oh, he was all about going in with guns blazing, but not without a plan to ensure he came out victorious—and alive. Taking Captain Searlington up on her offer was the smart play on many levels. He wouldn't have to worry about fucking up this investigation or worrying about if he was the right cop for this job. He'd be free of Camden and the sexy web the man spun as naturally as he drew breath. Agreeing to be removed might be the best course of action for them both.

But the sight of him wearing Elijah's T-shirt and sweatpants, looking less intimidating and more vulnerable without the armor of his three-piece suit, and Elijah hesitated to respond.

"Did you hear me, Stephenson?" Captain Searlington asked. "I'll have someone relieve you tonight, and you can be done with this."

There was his ticket out. All Elijah needed to do now was take it. He tried to say yes again, but Camden started biting his bottom lip, as if he somehow knew

Elijah was about to ditch him and his case. It would've been fitting. Elijah walking out with no more notice than Camden gave him all those years ago.

"Nah," Elijah replied as he hoped he wouldn't regret this hasty decision. Camden might be a pretentious asshole who probably deserved more than an ass-kicking or two. But he didn't deserve to live in fear of his life. "Don't worry about it. I'm good till it's done."

He ended the call, folding his arms casually over his chest, wondering why he hadn't taken the easy way out. It would've been so simple to walk away from this assignment. An assignment Elijah knew would cost him grief either professionally or personally. Maybe even both if his luck didn't hold out.

A quick glance at Camden, and Elijah noticed his charge had stopped biting his lip long enough to muster up a weary smile. The smile was weak and tentative, as if Camden were silently asking Elijah for something. In that moment, Elijah instantly knew why he'd chosen to stay. Camden needed him. He'd made Camden a promise to protect him. It was a promise Elijah knew he had to keep, even to his own detriment.

Too afraid to dig deeper, he walked to where Camden stood and clapped him on his shoulder. "Come on," Elijah murmured. "Let's go see what's on TV."

When Camden seemed confused and didn't follow behind Elijah in the hallway, Elijah turned to look back over his shoulder. "Hurry before I change my mind about letting you have my remote."

Chapter Seven

CAMDEN was bored. There was no other way to describe it. He'd been in captivity—or quaintly phrased—protective custody for only a few hours, and there was nothing left to do within these walls. Well, there was, but he was tired of watching TV. Anything else he might have been interested in doing was strictly forbidden by Lieutenant Pain-In-The-Ass. He couldn't use any of his virtual accounts because logging in would give anyone looking for him their location. No social media, no reading from his e-reader app, hell, he couldn't even log into work and reference anything in the law library. There was nothing to do, and the pervasive silence would drive Camden out of his mind.

He looked through the last sports magazine Elijah had lying around and tossed it on the coffee table. "How the hell does he stay here in all this quiet without going insane?"

"Who says I'm not already insane?"

Elijah's unexpected presence in the room made Camden jump from his reclined position on the couch while clutching his hand against his chest to soothe his startled heart.

"Can you please stop with the ninja-stealth steps? You will give me a heart attack," he shouted. "Then the Path to Unity won't have to worry about killing me off."

"Makes my job easier either way," Elijah responded as he shrugged his shoulder and sat on the sofa next to Camden. "If you're bored, why don't you come downstairs and work out with me?"

"We just had breakfast for dinner," Camden whined as he plopped his feet on top of the coffee table, cringing from the annoying sound of his own voice. He wasn't usually this high-maintenance, but even he had his limits. He was going stir-crazy. "Can't we relax?"

Elijah leaned forward, pushing Camden's feet off the coffee table as he stood up. "Suit yourself. I'll be in the basement working off some of the tightness in my leg if you need me."

Camden watched Elijah amble out of the room with an almost unnoticeable limp, and his inner toddler regretted the tantrum he'd just thrown. Elijah was working through pain to keep his body ready to protect Camden's life. And while he did that, Camden was behaving like a child who needed to be entertained every second of the day. It was petty and beneath a man of his import.

Camden could hear his mother admonishing him. *"Camden Nicholas Warren,"* she'd huff. *"Where are your manners? We must always be gracious to our hosts."* She'd be disappointed in his behavior, at least until she found out Elijah was a cop from a middle-class family with no legacy that the Warren pedigree would speak of. Then, her tune would probably change. Then she'd curl up her lip the way she did when she encountered something unsavory and say, *"Camden, please stop dallying with someone so obviously beneath our station. It reflects poorly on us, dear."*

As did most things that veered from the approved list of things Camden could do with his life as far as it concerned his parents.

Too bored to remain where he was and too frightened to venture beyond Elijah's home, Camden chose the only option left to him: working out in the basement with Elijah.

Camden expected to see Elijah lifting weights when he reached the bottom of the landing. Instead he found him sitting on the floor, leaning over the leg he'd been favoring upstairs, with his body almost flattened against the length. Camden would've stopped to enjoy the picture if he hadn't seen the wince of pain in the reflective surface of the mirror Elijah was sitting in front of.

"Hey." Camden spoke carefully as he stepped closer to Elijah's position inside the room. "You all right?"

"Yeah, I forgot to do my PT stretches for my leg this morning. It gets a little stiff if I don't stretch at least once a day since…."

"Since the attack?"

Elijah stopped stretching to look at Camden, his face colored with disbelief and a healthy dose of suspicion. "That's the second time you've asked me about something you either shouldn't care about or shouldn't have known about since we haven't spoken in the last five years. You keeping tabs? Or did you dismiss my order to stay off electronics, and google me?"

Camden didn't answer at first. Instead, he sat down on the floor opposite Elijah, and stretched his legs as far open as he could without dislocating his hips. He motioned for Elijah to do the same. When they each secured their hands to the other's forearms, Camden leaned back, pulling Elijah into a deep partner stretch for as long as Elijah could tolerate it.

"You gonna answer my question, Counselor?"

"Elijah, I work for the Brooklyn DA's office. I don't think it would be that farfetched I'd know about your attack. My office prosecuted the people responsible."

It was true, Camden's office had prosecuted and convicted the two lowlives responsible for almost killing Elijah. The case had come across Camden's desk. But when he recognized the name of the victim, he passed it off to another prosecutor. His father had been furious. It was a high-profile case guaranteed to garner media attention and raise his professional profile, if successfully prosecuted. But Camden knew he was too close to the case. He didn't want to risk the assailants beating the charge on a technicality. Instead, he flexed his muscles as the executive assistant district attorney and assigned it to one of his subordinates while closely supervising from behind the scenes.

"I was sorry to hear what happened to you, Elijah."

It was the truth. A milder version of the panic that flooded him upon learning of the attack. He'd even followed Lindsey to the hospital, pretending it was in an official capacity, even when he'd known Lindsey was there as Elijah's friend.

Camden took a breath, his frustration over his inability to be truthful with Elijah—and himself—weighing against his shoulders and chest. He stood up, walking to the massage table, or the hard slab of elevated wood with a body pillow atop it that doubled as a massage table, and motioned for Elijah to follow him.

"When my mom broke her leg a few years ago, her physical therapist would always rub her down after her workouts. Maybe a massage would help with your stiffness."

Elijah, still sitting on the floor, turned his head in Camden's direction, his mouth slightly agape as he prepared to speak.

Camden raised his hand, shaking an accusing finger at Elijah. "Get your mind out of the gutter, Lieutenant. I'm offering a therapeutic massage only."

"And the other kind isn't therapeutic?" Elijah's feigned innocence made Camden's pulse jump. This lighthearted side to the serious police officer was familiar, drawing Camden in so completely.

Elijah maneuvered himself off of the floor and ambled the few steps to the table. He sat down, lowering himself to the table, never taking his eyes off Camden as he did.

Even in jest, there was something so intense about those deep brown eyes. Then and now, Camden found it impossible to turn away from them whenever Elijah had his gaze leveled at him.

Camden was about to lay his hand flat against Elijah's clothed thigh, but then he caught what appeared to be apprehension in Elijah's eyes. "I will not hurt you, Elijah." The tenderness in his voice surprised Camden.

Not one to play nursemaid to anyone, he couldn't figure out the reason he was being so gentle with the strong man before him.

Maybe it was because he'd been such a jackass upstairs, or maybe it was because he didn't think it was smart to piss off the person charged with protecting you. Whatever it was, Camden needed to reassure Elijah of his motives.

"You can't hurt me, Camden," Elijah whispered before he closed his eyes and settled into Camden's touch. "You never could."

Elijah's Adam's apple bobbed as the man swallowed, and Camden wondered if it was a sign of nervousness. Was Elijah lying, or was he simply in pain from overworking the muscles in his leg? *Why would he lie? What could you have meant to him after one night?*

A chill spilled down Camden's spine. He stood frozen for a second, not sure why Elijah's statement made him feel so numb inside. They weren't longtime lovers; they were a one-night stand. They'd had a good time while they were together and owed each other nothing once it was over. That's the way all one-night stands happened.

But Camden would be lying if it hadn't nicked a small part of his soul that hoped and believed Elijah had mourned the loss of Camden. Because deep down, in the quiet of the night, when Camden was alone with himself, he mourned Elijah. Or more specifically, he mourned the promise of Elijah.

He didn't know him well enough to actually know Elijah. But that night, the potential of what Camden's life would be like if he could choose his own path, choose this man, it broke a small part of him that he kept hidden away from the rest of the world.

ELIJAH lost himself in Camden's therapeutic touch. He was slightly surprised when Camden offered to help. As self-centered as Elijah believed him to be, it seemed out of character that Camden would know anything about using his hands to help someone else. The way Elijah pegged him, writing a check was more Camden's speed than actually getting involved.

Camden was quiet as he worked through the knots in Elijah's leg, kneading each muscle into submission until the cramping sensation dissipated. By the time he finished, Elijah's leg was loose, and his body was warm with relaxation.

Elijah opened his eyes and turned to Camden to extend his thanks when he saw the sullen set of Camden's jaw and the distant look in his eyes. Concern made Elijah sit up and place a hand on Camden's forearm to stop him from walking away.

"What's wrong?"

He shook his head, trying to move away again when Elijah pulled him back. Elijah stood, and the length of their bodies touched, drawing a groan from Elijah.

Elijah had kept his response to Camden under control by picturing the perky little blonde woman who tortured him during his recovery. Despite her petite stature, she'd proven to be more than a match for Elijah's surly mood and his bullish demeanor. Every time Camden touched him, Elijah would hear Tina screaming at him, "Either you focus on your PT, or things get ugly."

But now, Tina's voice was nowhere to be found as the electric heat of excitement sizzled through him, making his senses come alive with need.

"This is a dangerous idea," Camden warned him while licking the tip of his tongue out slightly to wet his lips. Elijah's senses slowed down the motion, allowing him to take in every inch of skin on Camden's mouth that tiny slip of tongue swept across.

Elijah sucked in a breath through widened nostrils, hoping to find a way to keep himself in check. Camden was right. This was a bad idea, and if Elijah didn't walk away now, he knew he'd lose the battle waging between his mind and his body over keeping his dick in his pants.

He closed his eyes, savoring the feel of Camden's proximity while simultaneously reprimanding himself for not stepping away. Removing himself from the situation would be the smart thing. Walking away the way Camden had would keep them both safe. Unfortunately, his brain clocked out at that exact moment, leaving Elijah with nothing but a long-denied need that demanded satisfaction.

You can do this, Stephenson. It was one night. That's all.

Elijah repeated that mantra in his head for a few more seconds, just long enough to convince himself he had this infatuation with Camden under control. But when Elijah's gaze locked with Camden's and he saw the wounded flicker of pain in the depths of the man's blue eyes, smart left the building, and his need to protect Camden took over.

He couldn't say exactly how it happened, but he buried his fingers into Camden's dark strands, pulling him into Elijah's arms.

Elijah placed gentle lips against Camden's temple, smiling as a quick shiver passed through him. Camden set his hand on Elijah's forearm, carefully leaning into the barely there kiss.

"Elijah," Camden whispered again. "This is such a bad idea."

He pressed his forehead to Camden's as he positioned both thumbs on either side of the man's jaw and moaned, "I know."

Chapter Eight

ELIJAH pressed gentle lips over Camden's mouth for a brief second. He pulled away and released the shaky breath he'd been holding. Electricity still lit up Elijah's senses like a torch when he touched Camden. It was disarming. What kind of man could cause so much need in Elijah with a caress of his lips?

The kind I need to stay away from.

Elijah's instincts were seldom wrong. His inner voice always kept him out of harm's way. Well, as long as he listened to it, it kept him out of trouble. Listening to that still, small voice that helped him discern whenever danger was near had spared his life a time or two. And yet now, even though it tugged at his mind, begging for his undivided attention, all Elijah could do was see the sexy lawyer in front of him. All he remembered was the sweet taste of Camden across his lips.

Elijah moaned aloud. The sound smothered the warning voice in his head. He tightened his fingers in Camden's hair, latching his mouth onto Camden's in a fierce press of lips against lips. If this would stop, and Elijah knew it should, Camden would have to be the one sensible enough to bring this to an end. But if the desperate way he kissed him back was any sign, Camden didn't seem to care about sensibility either.

If either of them had been thinking straight, instead of just responding to the need their frenzied touches created, they'd have made the few steps it would've taken to reach the guest bedroom on the other end of the basement. There was a couch and a bed there, a cushioned place for them to devour each other against. But the fire threatening to consume Elijah rendered the thought of moving painful. The massage table pressing into the back of his thighs would have to be good enough. It was that or the floor, and his recently aching leg put the kibosh on that idea the second it tried to form in Elijah's mind.

During the brief instant Elijah had taken to map out where this could take place, Camden's hands snaked down his chest and continued traveling until they reached Elijah's waistband.

"Eager much?" Elijah didn't need for Camden to answer his question. The way his shaky fingers were pushing at Elijah's sweatpants solidified the notion that Camden desired him. Elijah smiled more to himself than Camden at the memory of how frank of a lover Camden was. If memory served, Camden had been enthusiastic to get Elijah naked their first time too.

Camden pushed Elijah's sweatpants down until the waistband met the middle of his thighs. He closed his fingers around Elijah's thickening cock and gave him an eager stroke.

"Shut up before good sense ruins this," Camden huffed. Elijah nodded his head and reached out to hook a finger behind the elastic of Camden's sweatpants and pushed them down enough to free Camden's cock.

Elijah closed his hand around Camden's cock, much the same as Camden had done to him. No finesse, no fanfare, just delicious pressure and warmth. As Camden released a needy moan, Elijah grabbed Camden's waist and pulled until their bodies were touching again.

"Come here," Elijah grunted as he hauled Camden tighter against him for another kiss.

Kissing wasn't something Elijah often engaged in with his sex partners. First, not everyone knew how. The worst thing in the world was a sloppy kisser who left your mouth and face feeling wet in that non-sexy kind of way. Second, even if they knew how, kissing required an intimacy Elijah rarely allowed between himself and the fucks he picked up here and there whenever the need arose. But kissing Camden was something spiritual. The way the softness of his lips met Elijah's press for press with just the right amount of pressure to make Elijah want to drink from this man's mouth for as long as he could connected to something deeper than just physical pleasure.

Each kiss ramped up the hunger growing in his belly. He could pretend the need coiling inside him like a tight spring was a surprise to him. But the truth was he'd been aching for this since he crossed paths with Camden in Captain Searlington's office. Even though he'd been foolish enough to think the desire this man sparked in him was something he could ignore or toss aside.

The tight squeeze of Camden's palm surrounding Elijah's flesh pulled a needy groan from his parted lips. Camden must have understood the nonverbal "More" buried in the animalistic sound, because he moved Elijah's hand from his own cock and gripped both of them together.

The feel of his dick pressed so closely to Camden's was nearly Elijah's undoing. He bit down into his lip, the sting preventing him from falling over into overwhelming pleasure.

"Close" was all Elijah could muster on a shaky breath. If he'd been with any other man, his lack of control would embarrass him. But when his gaze locked with Camden's, he saw the same need, the same desperation in the tight muscles of Camden's neck and face. He wasn't the only one being swept under the strong tow of desire. Camden was right there with him.

The only thing Elijah cared about was feeling the slide of Camden's hand around him, and how satisfying his release would be.

Two more strokes, and the familiar tingle sparked at the bottom of his spine. His muscles tensed, and the electric wave of passion bloomed and spread through his nerve endings. His balls pulled up tight, and his breath locked in his chest as the first jet of his cum released and landed on Camden's hand.

If he'd been in control of his body, he would've watched as Camden spilled over into oblivion right after him. He would've reveled in the hungry sounds Camden was making as his cock pulsed next to Elijah's. If he'd been able to do anything but surrender to the wave of pleasure he was drowning in, he'd have swallowed those delicious sounds Camden was making with a desperate kiss that left them both gasping for air. But he was too wrapped up in the sensations Camden's touch garnered, so all he could do was brace himself against the massage table and hope not to fall to the floor like a rock.

Camden fell against Elijah's chest with a hard thump, knocking them both onto the massage table in an awkward pile.

They were sticky with sweat and quickly cooling cum. If there was ever a picture of a disheveled mess, Elijah was certain they fit the bill. But no matter how much of a mess they were, relief and comfort spread through him, soothing him in ways that would make Elijah uncomfortable if he thought about it long enough.

But the soft kisses Camden placed against his cheek and the lazy way the man ran his fingers through Elijah's loose locs made it impossible for Elijah to think about anything other than the satisfaction Camden's touch gave him.

Camden was never to be more than what he'd been, a quick fuck for one night in his distant past. But now and then, even their thin ties or lack of acquaintanceship didn't mask what had always been. With the least amount of effort, Camden had an innate ability to make Elijah's body tremble.

Elijah should be ashamed of that. His lack of control should disgust him. He was a cop. A trained officer of the law. If he couldn't control himself, then who could?

He'd regret it tomorrow. He knew he would. How could he not? Their complicated history added to the current issue of Camden's safety meant becoming sexually involved with Camden would cost him more grief than he'd want to consider. But in this moment, the only thing his mind wondered was how long before they could do that again.

He was so fucked.

Chapter Nine

IN his peripheral vision Elijah caught a quick glance of Camden stepping out of the basement bathroom and fixing his clothing. He knew he should say something. But he didn't think "Thanks for the hand job, but that can never happen again" would go down well five seconds after they'd peeled themselves apart.

So instead of manning up right then and there, Elijah took his turn in the bathroom to clean away the evidence of their mistake. He washed his hands and tried to avoid his reflection in the mirror. Too ashamed to look at himself, he sucked in a deep breath and resolved to put on his big boy pants and say what he needed to say.

He opened the door, straightening his back, trying to find the strength to speak. "Camden—" Camden lifted his hand, cutting his words short.

"Is this the part where you tell me that was a mistake? Because if it is, save it. We're both adults, we both wanted it."

Elijah nodded. Camden wasn't using tricky lawyer speak to mince words. It was direct, clear truth. Elijah had wanted every minute. But his desire for Camden didn't change the facts of their situation. Camden was off-limits. Elijah just needed to convince them both of that.

"It still needs to be said, though. This can't happen again. I fucked up in letting it happen now. If anyone ever found out, I'd lose my badge. If something happened to you because I was off my game... there's just too much that could go wrong. Camden, I—"

Whatever he was about to say died on his tongue when he heard a creak in the above floorboards that rattled him. He stepped closer to Camden and put a hand over his mouth, signaling Camden to be silent. Elijah kept his hand over Camden's lips, searching for the faint sound that had tripped his internal panic button.

Elijah waited a beat, hoping he imagined the slight disturbance, the usual noises of a house settling. But the slow creak of wooden floors bearing weight above him sent Elijah's cop senses into overdrive.

He removed his hand from Camden's mouth and hastened to a hidden panel in a nearby wall. He pressed against it and dialed the numeric code into the waiting keypad. When the lock tumbled open, he pulled the lever on the safe door, and removed a holster. In one smooth motion, it was around his shoulders. Next, he removed a loaded Glock from the safe.

He reached inside the safe again and picked up a pair of handcuffs and car keys. He shoved the handcuffs in his pockets and handed the car keys to Camden.

"Stay here while I check it out. If you hear gunfire, I want you to leave through the cellar doors, go over my fence into my neighbor's yard, and access the street. You should find a dark blue sedan right in front of their house. Keep driving until you find a cop or a precinct. Do not come back looking for me."

Camden's eyes were wide with shock and apprehension. "But what about you?"

Elijah shook his head. "Don't worry about me. If you need to, run, Camden."

Camden finally nodded his head. Elijah took one final, filling look at him and then moved up the stairs.

He slid his back against the wall when he reached the top of the staircase and tightened his grip on his weapon. Cold fear spread through him as he prepared to turn the corner and face the threat. A gun in his hand had never felt as heavy in his palm as it did now. A shiver of anxiety passed through him, making him glance back the way he'd come. Part of him begged him to follow Camden instead of playing hero.

He was halfway resolved to do just that, but then he remembered the fear he'd seen painted across Camden's face earlier in the day, and couldn't walk away. If he ran, Camden would never be safe.

Elijah took a quiet breath and steadied himself. If this motherfucker was bold enough to step inside Elijah's home, then Elijah had to be bold enough to protect Camden.

When he heard the intruder take another step toward the basement stairs, Elijah stepped into the dark hallway, aimed his gun at the head of the shadowy figure, and yelled, "Freeze, NYPD!"

The silhouette instantly stopped moving.

"Get on your knees and keep your fucking hands where I can see them, or I'll blow a hole in your goddamn head!"

His heart pounded in his chest as he neared the intruder. Just because a man was on his knees didn't mean he wasn't dangerous. He stepped carefully until he reached the intruder, then grabbed one of his arms and tugged it behind his back as he planted his gun at the base of his skull.

"Facedown on the floor right now!"

The intruder complied, easing himself onto the floor with the help of Elijah's knee pressing in his back. When the man was facedown, Elijah tucked the gun into his holster. He quickly handcuffed the perpetrator and yanked him up from the floor, slamming him against the wall.

Elijah pulled his gun out again, training it on the intruder before reaching out and turning on the light. He blinked as his eyes adjusted, and cringed when he saw the intruder's face.

"What the fuck are you doing, Emmanuel?"

Elijah dropped the hand with his gun to his side as he focused on his younger brother's face. "Do you realize I could've killed you? Why are you sneaking around my damn house?"

His brother, the same height and burly build as Elijah with a shaved head, a thin goatee, and sandalwood complexion, cocked his right brow and tilted his head.

"Exactly which of those questions would you like me to answer first, big brother? Is there any particular order you'd like them answered?"

Elijah squinted his eyes as he leveled his gaze at his brother. "Don't be cute, Manny. I could've killed you. You know you're always supposed to call before showing up at my place. Let me fucking know to expect your trifling ass before you step up into my crib."

"I told you last week Vivienne, me, and the 'rents were coming up here to spend a long weekend with your grouchy ass, celebrate you going back to work."

Elijah shook his head as he pointed a finger at his brother. "Bullshit, Manny! You told me y'all were thinking about heading up here this weekend or the next. I clearly remember you telling me you'd call me to let me know if it was a go."

His brother's features tightened into a perfect mix of anger and annoyance. "E. I called you Wednesday and told you we'd be here sometime Friday for the weekend. You said you had to go to your station, on either Thursday or Friday. You were still waiting for a call from your captain. If you weren't here when we arrived, let myself in."

"Shit." Elijah passed his free hand down the length of his locs and shook his head. He had spoken to Emmanuel on Wednesday. That was before all hell broke loose and he was saddled with a protection detail. "Fine, I got my days mixed up, but that still doesn't explain why you were sneaking around in here. Your steps were too careful."

"Your SUV isn't in the driveway or anywhere on this block, yet the lights were on in your basement. I was checking to make sure nobody ran up in your shit. Now, would you mind taking these fucking cuffs off me before my wife and our mama walk in here?"

Elijah turned his head toward a backyard-facing window and saw movement in his carport. Just what he fucking needed, a house full of family when he was hiding Camden Warren in his basement.

"How long y'all staying?"

"Till Monday evening. We each took a day off. Mama was insistent we spend this time together before you disappeared into that precinct again."

Shame bled through Elijah. His mother's assumption wasn't wrong. Going back to work would cut into their family time. But once this ordeal was over with Camden, his desk job wouldn't impose such demands on his time. He'd be a better son and brother this time around. He just needed to get beyond Monday, and everything would be all right.

"The keys are downstairs," he growled through clenched teeth, slipped the gun in the holster, and walked past his brother, his footfalls heavy on each stair to warn Camden of his arrival.

When he entered the basement, a brief glance revealed an empty room absent of Camden. Panic pulled at the base of his skull. Did Camden leave? Was he out there alone on the streets in harm's way, all for a silly misunderstanding with Elijah's inconsiderate brother?

"Camden, it's me," Elijah announced as he stepped farther into the open room. "You still here, man?"

The closet door opened, and Camden stepped into the room. Relief curved Elijah's lips into a half smile until he saw the grayish tint to Camden's skin and the frantic way Camden's eyes were darting back and forth.

Almost every interaction Elijah had with the man revealed Camden to be a cocky asshole. Sickeningly self-assured and resolute in his belief that his smarts, his title, his pedigree made him untouchable. But standing in front of Elijah now, Camden resembled nothing of his former self. Camden was scared.

Elijah met him in the middle of the room and cupped a hand to his face. "Hey," he whispered, hoping to soothe the panic flowing through Camden. "It was just my silly-ass kid brother. They haven't found us. You're fine."

Camden pressed his face into Elijah's palm, responding more to the tactile stimuli than the verbal. "Everything's fine."

Camden closed his eyes for a beat, then opened them. He searched Elijah's gaze for assurance. He swallowed, then cleared his throat before speaking. "Are you certain, Elijah?"

"Well, we're not in any physical danger. But there is an issue we need to deal with."

Elijah could see the question forming between Camden's pinched brows. He opened his mouth to inform him of the proverbial monkey wrench in their plans, also known as his family. But before the first word could leave his tongue, he heard footsteps on the stairs and his brother's boisterous voice filling the air.

"A-yo, E. Stop playing and take these damn cuffs off me?"

When Emmanuel stumbled closer, he stopped just short of where Elijah and Camden were standing and zeroed in on Elijah's hand against Camden's cheek.

Emmanuel lifted a knowing brow and grinned like a teenaged boy before speaking. "My bad, E. I didn't know you had—" Emmanuel paused for a long second and nodded his head toward Camden. "—company."

Chapter Ten

ELIJAH dropped his hand quickly and turned to his brother. "That's what happens when you don't call before you drop by."

Elijah excused himself to retrieve the handcuff keys from the safe. He removed the restraints, throwing them and the keys back in the safe. He then pulled his gun and holster off, sliding them next to the keys before relocking the safe door.

"I did call," Emmanuel answered. "Not my fault senility is setting in early." He smiled as he looked back and forth between Elijah and Camden. "So, you're not going to introduce me to your guest?" Elijah's lip curled as he watched the gleam shining on his brother's face. Since they were kids, Emmanuel had lived to make life difficult for Elijah. Finding him in what could only have appeared to be a cozy moment between two well-acquainted people was just the ammunition a needling little brother would pounce on. It didn't matter that both Elijah and his brother were grown and in their thirties. Emmanuel would always be Elijah's pain-in-the-ass brother.

"This is Camden." Elijah pointed to the middle of the room where Camden stood and watched as his brother walked over and extended a hand in greeting.

"Hi, Camden. I'm Elijah's brother, Emmanuel. Most people call me Manny."

Camden smiled, and Elijah noticed it didn't reach his eyes. When Camden shared a genuine smile, his eyes sparkled with intelligence and his easy sense of humor. This was a professional smile, one you put in place even when you didn't feel like smiling in front of the world.

"Hello, Manny, it's a pleasure to meet you." The polite tone in Camden's voice grated on Elijah's nerves. He didn't understand why. Camden's tone wasn't bracing, but it wasn't warm and welcoming either. To Elijah, this was Camden's show voice, and after hearing the raw guttural sounds their joint orgasms pulled from Camden, this facsimile was a poor imitation to Elijah's ears.

"I didn't know Elijah had a brother."

"I'm not surprised he didn't mention me." Elijah narrowed his eyes as he watched his brother move closer to Camden. "I'm the sexier, more successful brother. He's afraid I'd steal all his dates."

Elijah waved a dismissive hand as he moved closer to Emmanuel. "Yeah, because every man wants to spend his time with a self-important, inconsiderate asshole like you. Right, Manny?" Elijah continued to glare at Emmanuel, locking gazes with him, returning hard stare for hard stare until Emmanuel cracked first, resulting in them both breaking into laughter.

Elijah had spoken the truth. His younger brother's ego straddled the line between confidence and conceit. He was self-absorbed, and Lord knew, he displayed the asshole gene that seemed to run rampant through the males of the Stephenson family more than either Elijah or their father. But no matter his shortcomings, Emmanuel was his brother, and Elijah was always glad to see him.

The two men clasped hands, pulling each other into a tight hug. "Manny." Elijah pointed to Camden before returning his gaze to his brother. "Would you give us a minute? I need to prepare Camden for the Stephenson tribe. We're a hard pill to swallow in large doses."

Emmanuel nodded and left them alone in the basement. Elijah waited a moment, making certain he heard Emmanuel's footsteps above them on the first floor.

"What are we going to do now that your family is here? It's not safe for them to be around me. What if these maniacs find me and your family is here, Elijah?" Camden rattled off his questions in quick succession, leaving no opportunity for Elijah to answer. His hands were planted against his trim waist, his shoulders high, his chest moving rapidly as he took large gulps of air.

There it was again. The panic that Camden stuffed down, keeping it hidden from the rest of the world. He'd seen a glimpse of it when they'd shared dinner over the kitchen counter. But now, it seemed to be too much for Camden to handle.

Elijah placed a calming but firm hand on one of Camden's shoulders, giving him something to anchor himself with.

"Hey," he murmured. "My father is an armed, retired cop. There isn't anyone better at protection than him. My brother isn't a cop, but he's run through Daddy Bootcamp just like I have; he's not helpless in a situation like this. And don't get me started on my mama and my sister-in-law. Those two are scary when they're pissed. I'd pity anyone who thought to darken their doorstep."

That last line seemed to bring Camden's gaze back into focus, giving way to a slight smile curling the corners of his mouth.

"If they're that tough, are we gonna tell them why I'm here?"

Elijah shook his head. "My dad maybe, but I don't want to ruin this weekend for my mother." Evelyn Stephenson had been Elijah's rock. She'd pulled Elijah every step of the way during his rehabilitation. Sometimes dragging him kicking and screaming when he couldn't muster the motivation to work at his own recovery.

She had worried about Elijah since the shooting. Knowing he was going back to a supposedly safe unit in the precinct was a relief for her. He wouldn't scare her by letting her know he was on a dangerous detail.

"Let's keep it simple, Camden." His father might be the ex-cop, but his mother and sister-in-law were top-notch investigators. Those two could smell a lie like a rat did cheese. If they went in with a convoluted scheme, they'd know it.

"Being too elaborate will get us caught. You're a friend visiting from out of town. I got my signals crossed with your travel dates." As long as Camden stuck to it, they should be in the clear.

Elijah watched Camden carefully as he shook his head. He seemed calmer; some of the tension in his shoulders seemed to bleed away as he dropped his hands from his waist. But there was still a sense of dread floating around him in the careful way he took slow, shallow breaths.

"The me being a friend visiting is a solid plan, Elijah. But still, this is your family we're talking about. I'm hiding from people who didn't think twice about putting a bomb under my car. Is it wise to keep me here?"

"We don't have much choice right now. Moving you is dangerous. It would probably take my captain a couple of days to mobilize a move for you anyway. Telling my family about you could be a risk too. They won't be here for long. We'll pretend to be besties for a few days, and they'll be on their way."

Camden rubbed a hand up and down against his opposite arm as if he was trying to brush a chill away. "If you think this is best, I'll go along with it."

"I know it is." Elijah motioned for Camden to follow him, and they both headed for the stairs. When they rounded the corner and stepped into the kitchen, Elijah's heart danced a little at the sight of the small, round woman with a cherub's smile and wide-open arms waiting for him to step into them.

"There's my favorite son," Evelyn sang as Elijah bent down, wrapped his arms around her waist, and lifted her off of the floor in a bear hug.

"You know I can hear you, right, Ma?" Emmanuel's comment went ignored by Evelyn as long as Elijah held her. He kissed his mother on the cheek, then placed her back on her feet as he gave his brother a smug smirk.

"Why be mad at the truth, Manny? I told you she loves me more. And we both know she's not the only one either."

Elijah stepped around his mother and into the arms of his sister-in-law, Vivienne. "Come here, girl, and give me some sugar." Elijah made an overexaggeration of his display of affection for Vivienne because he knew it ticked his brother off.

With a close-faded Caesar haircut that accentuated her high cheekbones and full, heart-shaped mouth, the brown-skinned beauty's affections were a prize his brother had been lucky to receive. "I was just telling my brother he ought to thank his lucky stars you were gracious enough to marry beneath your station, because we both know who got the better deal in this marriage contract."

She giggled and waved a hand at him. "Elijah, are you sure you're not checking for us ladies? You've got better game than any straight man who's tried to kick it to me before. You should teach a class."

"I did," Elijah answered with a playful wink of his eye. "How do you think my brother pulled your card?"

"Elijah, stop flirting with your brother's wife." Elijah's smile grew wider as he turned to embrace his father.

"But, Pops," Elijah answered, "it's so much fun."

His father matched Elijah's wide grin with one of his own as he pulled Elijah in for a hug.

Walter Stephenson carried the same height and build as his sons, tall, solid, strong, and unmovable in most things. But when it came to loving his family, the older man took advantage of every opportunity he had to show them they meant everything to him.

Walter ran a hand down the length of Elijah's locs and smiled again. "I see Captain Searlington still hasn't made you cut all that hair off."

"Nope." Elijah grinned. "She knows I'd sooner turn in my badge."

"You sound awful confident you're worth all that grief I know you're bringing her."

Elijah shrugged his shoulder. "I am my daddy's son. They don't make 'em like us Stephenson boys."

"Damn right, son, they sure don't."

His father clamped his hand on Elijah's shoulder and pointed to the doorway.

"Now, one of these things is not like the other, Elijah."

Elijah already knew where this was going, and the hair on his arms stood up in anticipation of his father's line of questioning.

This was how interrogations had always begun in Elijah's house as a child. First his father would come to him with a playful, disarming tone that lulled Elijah and his brother into a false sense of security. Once his father had fattened them up for the kill, he'd tag their mother in for the win, and she'd decimate any lie he and his brother had cooked up.

Keep it cool, and everything'll be fine.

"No worries, Pops." Elijah kept his breathing even and his smile tempered as he glanced at Camden standing in the kitchen doorway.

Much to Elijah's surprise, Camden was leaning against the doorjamb, arms crossed against his chest, one ankle overlapping the other. He wore an amused smile that made him look carefree. His blue eyes sparked with laughter, and the laid-back picture he made reminded Elijah of their one night of conversation and lovemaking.

"Elijah." His father's voice intruding on his thoughts brought him out of his musings. "You were saying?"

Elijah shook his head and cleared his throat, giving himself a little time to put his game face back on.

"Pops." His voice cracked a little again. Determined to sound like the grown-ass man he was, Elijah cleared his throat again and willed his voice to remain steady. "Everyone. This is my friend Camden. We'd made plans a while ago for him to hang out up here, but I completely spaced on the dates. It didn't dawn on me that you guys would be here this weekend."

There was silence in the room; all eyes seemed to be on Camden, then on him. All Elijah had to do was keep it together, and the rest of the weekend would flow smoothly.

Finally breaking the silence, his mother pulled her gaze away from Camden and leveled it at Elijah. "Your friend?" The careful lilt to her voice painted the air with suspicion. "Elijah, I'm not that old that I can't see what's going on here."

"Mama, I promise you—"

"We've messed around and stumbled into a lover's getaway. Why didn't you tell us you had plans with someone special?"

Before Elijah could process what was happening, his mother walked up to Camden, spread her arms wide, and wrapped them around Camden's middle.

"It's so nice to meet someone my boy feels is special enough to bring home."

"Mama—"

Elijah tried to interrupt, but his mother dismissed him with a wave of her hand and a "Boy, hush," before she turned to Elijah's father with an ear-to-ear grin.

"Walter, our baby has finally got him a man to bring home."

The floor of his stomach plummeted, and he had to breathe through pursed lips to keep its contents from climbing up his esophagus.

The thought of his mother gushing about his love life and a man he'd just received a magnificent hand job from only moments before would sicken anyone. Add the fact that said man walked out on him without a second thought, and it was a wonder Elijah didn't empty his stomach in the middle of the kitchen floor.

"And Walter." The conspiratorial gleam in her eye made Elijah's heart rate race. "He's a cute one too."

Please, God. Please kill me now.

Chapter Eleven

CAMDEN stood in the kitchen doorway with both arms filled with Elijah's mother. It should've been uncomfortable. People in his circles didn't wrap themselves around perfect strangers and squeeze with all their strength. Although the older woman had taken Camden by surprise with the force of her affection, the warmth blossoming inside his chest made being angry or uncomfortable with Evelyn's lack of personal boundaries impossible.

If he were to be honest—something his life or his work rarely permitted—being held by this stranger made him feel at ease in a way he couldn't quite recognize.

Camden lifted his eyes from the armful of Elijah's mother he was holding and saw the lines of Elijah's jaw tighten.

Oh, somebody's not liking this at all.

For a beat Camden thought of backing off. Poking the bear when the bear was responsible for your safety probably wasn't a wise thing. But resisting a challenge wasn't in Camden's nature. His need to not just win, but to decimate his opponent, was one of the reasons he was such a good trial lawyer. Aside from suborning perjury, there wasn't much Camden wouldn't do to win a case.

He watched Elijah's eyes narrow into tiny slits and opted to ignore the obvious warning the brooding police officer was silently throwing across the room.

"Mrs. Stephenson, please forgive Elijah." Camden gave Elijah's mother one last squeeze of his arms, then stepped out of her embrace to look down into her warm, smiling face.

She shared the same deep, rich brown tone as Elijah. And although her sons clearly inherited their tall, burly frames from their father, the full smile, the appled cheeks, the quick wit, it was all hers. "He wasn't expecting me this weekend. Work sort of dropped me in his lap."

She wrinkled her nose at him to feign disappointment, but the cheerful smile hiding in her eyes told Camden it was all a show. "Don't tell me you're a workaholic like my Elijah?"

Camden took both her hands and placed a sweet kiss on them. "I'm afraid I'd be lying to you if I said otherwise."

Still smiling, she shook her head. "If you work anywhere near as much as Elijah used to, it's a wonder the two of you ever see each other."

If Camden and Elijah were in a relationship, Evelyn's estimation would be correct. The DA's office swallowed huge chunks of Camden's time. You didn't make executive ADA as quickly as he did without sacrificing a personal life.

Sure, it would've been nice to have someone to share his time with, but if you wanted something extraordinary, sacrifices had to be made.

A chill filled his chest as he remembered his father repeating those exact words to Camden. *God, I'm even quoting him in my head.*

Refusing to let his father dampen his amusement, Camden refocused on Evelyn, leaning into her slightly, gracing her with a smile of his own. "We make it work. When it's important, when he's important, you make it work."

Camden made the mistake of raising his gaze from the smiling woman's face in search of her son's. Sure, this entire conversation was a charade. But the tight pull in his stomach when his gaze connected with the steady, intentional stare Elijah returned was as real as the breath caught in Camden's chest.

Maybe you really shouldn't poke the bear.

"**ELIJAH,** come help me haul the rest of your mama's junk in from the car."

"Junk?" Evelyn countered. "Most of that is food you're gonna shove in your mouth, Walter. You ought to be grateful I made a grocery run before we left. You know this child don't keep no food in the house."

Elijah locked his gaze on Camden's captivating blue eyes. Sure, he heard his mother and father bickering somewhere in the distance, but his focus couldn't spare his parents even a glimmer of attention.

Camden was smiling and laughing with Elijah's mother right at his side, and all Elijah could focus on was how perfect this all would be if it were real. If things had turned out differently in the past, they may well have shared a weekend like this with Elijah's family.

"Elijah." His father's baritone interrupted the living daydream Elijah was enthralled by. "You coming?"

Elijah took one more glance at Camden and broke free of the connection only the two of them seemed to be aware of in the room. When he stepped outside into the cool air, it was a pleasant relief. Be it anger, frustration, or desire, Camden had the ability to make Elijah's blood boil. A fact Elijah had to get control over if he was going to keep Camden safe.

When Elijah met his father at the back of the SUV, his father turned to him and asked, "What the fuck was that about?"

"Camden is—"

"Elijah, we both know Camden isn't your man. What exactly did we interrupt?"

He was about to answer his father when a question popped into his head. "Wait, what makes you think he isn't mine?"

"Because you brought him home."

Elijah wasn't exactly certain what his father's statement meant. He may not have settled down over the years, but he hadn't lived like a hermit either. He'd enjoyed a healthy run of men in his bed over the years. What the hell was his father getting at?

"I don't follow."

Walter Stephenson crossed his arms over his chest and widened his stance. "Elijah, you bring men to that apartment in Brooklyn like it has a revolving door. In tonight, gone tomorrow."

"True," he agreed even though his father's words still puzzled him. "So, why is it so strange I've brought Camden here?"

"Because the apartment in Brooklyn is where you sleep." Walter pointed his finger back toward Elijah's house. "But that house is your home, Elijah. And if a man was serious enough for you to let into your home, there's no way your mother and I would find out about him like this."

He swallowed, thrown off his game by his father's observation. Elijah didn't dispute his father's words. He knew without thinking, or even trying to calculate, that the only people who'd entered his home were service people and his family. No friends, no acquaintances, and certainly no dates.

"So, tell me"—the rumble of his father's voice in his ear made Elijah twitch slightly—"why is the executive ADA cozying up to my wife in your kitchen?"

Elijah took a deep breath and gently chewed on the inside of his bottom lip. He had a choice here. He could continue to push this ridiculous notion of him and Camden being a couple, or he could come clean. There were consequences to both paths.

Lying had never been Elijah's strong suit. When you were told it didn't matter what anyone else thought, that as long as you weren't hurting anyone else, your life was your own to live as you pleased, lying didn't seem all that necessary a skill to have.

His parents raised Elijah to live out loud, to embrace and walk in his truth. His parents had given him that gift. As a black, gay little boy growing up in the 'hood in East New York, Brooklyn, his life could've played out differently than it had. But because Elijah never believed he had to apologize for belonging to any of those demographics, he moved through the world with a sense of authority that told him he didn't have to lie about who and what he was and where he came from.

One would think that after fourteen years on the force, and a large portion of that time being spent in undercover work, would make Elijah the greatest liar there was. But what most didn't understand about undercover police work was that the best cover was built from the truth.

Elijah straightened his shoulders and looked his father in the eye before speaking. This was the man who not only taught Elijah about truth and justice but exemplified those characteristics in practice. If he wanted the truth, Elijah would give it to him.

"Pops, you guys stumbled in on a case I'm working." Elijah could see the confusion settling in his father's eyes, but before he could speak, Elijah pushed forward with his explanation. "I know I was supposed to be sitting behind a desk when I did return to work. But the powers that be demanded I take on one last case in the field. I've got to protect Camden from a cult group that's trying to kill him before he makes it to trial next week."

Elijah's father leaned against the vehicle and took in a deep breath. After digesting Elijah's explanation, Walter stood up and focused on Elijah again.

"So, you brought him to your house, Elijah? How does that make sense?"

Elijah laughed. It was true; there was a risk in him bringing Camden here, more than one in fact, and not all having to do with this case.

"This house isn't attached to me, not on the surface anyway." Elijah had purchased this house through a shell company he'd created. One couldn't work in Vice for as long as he did and not walk away with more than a handful of enemies. If those enemies could find his name easily on a property record, Elijah wouldn't have survived as long as he had in the game. "Not to mention, technically, I'm still on the disability list. There's nothing on paper that connects me to Camden or the precinct right now. If they're looking for him, my spot is the last place they'll look."

His father nodded. Elijah could see acquiescence taking hold in Walter's eyes as the man mulled over Elijah's explanation. "It's not the most orthodox plan you could've come up with, son. Who knows where you have him?"

Elijah shook his head. "No one. My captain knows I have him, but she doesn't know where. I'm not using my cell, only contacting the captain through a burner."

His father continued to nod his head as he processed the info Elijah was feeding him. "You know your mama can't know about this, right?"

Elijah's chest swelled with discomfort. Choosing not to disclose the particulars of his dangerous job was one thing. Allowing her to believe her son had found love, something he knew she prayed for, was a different scenario. The image of her wrapping herself around Camden both frightened and excited him at the same time. It was a glimpse into a future he'd hoped his new desk job would help him build.

But that future couldn't happen with Camden. And no matter how ready his mother seemed to designate Camden her extra son, the reality was Camden would walk away from Elijah when this was all over. If he perpetuated this lie, it would disappoint his mother.

But what was the alternative?

"She'd worry."

His father sighed loudly and rubbed the sides of his temple. "Between my twenty years on the force, and your fourteen, and nearly losing you, Elijah, her heart can't take it. She's a strong woman. She'd have to be to put up with me all these years. But your mother pushed herself so much worrying about you in that hospital bed and during your recovery that her heart nearly gave out."

Elijah didn't need the memory of finding his mother on the floor unresponsive and laboring to breathe as a reminder of how deadly stress could be. The doctor had called it a small heart attack. Nothing about its effects seemed small to Elijah. A change in diet, more exercise, and minimal stress had been the recommendation. His mother had dedicated her life to taking care of the men in her family. And in kind, the three Stephenson men vowed they'd do whatever they needed to keep Evelyn Stephenson alive and thriving.

"She's gonna kill me when she finds out Camden and I are scamming her." Elijah moved next to his father, nudging him slightly out of the way as he leaned against the SUV. "And then she's gonna kill you when she finds out you knew about it."

His father chuckled and shook his head. "You ain't ever lied, son."

Walter pushed off from the car and began a slow saunter toward the stairs leading to the house, leaving Elijah to replay their conversation in his head. It wasn't until his father reached the top of the landing that Elijah realized what was bothering him.

"How did you know Camden was the executive ADA? I never mentioned that. And as far as I know,

PD has kept his attack under wraps from the press. The explosion was linked to a faulty gas pump, and no injuries or casualties were revealed."

Walter turned around to answer Elijah's question. His brow furrowed into a sharp point between his eyebrows. "I met him at the hospital when you were attacked."

"He was there?"

Elijah's memory of that time was still sketchy. Between the pain meds and the brain swelling, Elijah couldn't trust any of the strange visions that haunted him from that time. But somewhere in the depths of his subconscious Elijah remembered a glimmer of Camden's face. He'd passed it off all this time as the wishful musings of a dying man. But what if he wasn't dreaming? What if Camden had been there?

"He was the first one from the DA's office to come to your hospital bed when you were attacked."

Elijah followed his father up the stairs, leaning against the banister as he sifted through his father's answer. "Then why didn't Mama and Manny recognize him?"

"Your mother and brother weren't with me when the squad car pulled up to the house. Manny and Viv were on vacation, and your mother was off on that missionary trip with her church in Boston. She arrived by police escort a few hours after me." Walter returned to the house as Elijah jogged back down the steps and removed the remaining suitcase from the SUV's cargo area.

Elijah had believed it was a dream all this time. Hell, even if Camden had been in his room, the memory Elijah carried with him could well have been a hallucination. Just his mind's way of easing Elijah's pain and giving him something to hold on to.

He tried to think back to that time. All of it was hazy to him. One minute Elijah was doing a dirty gun

deal in the back room of an underground club. The next, he was blocking an attack from multiple directions. It was dark, and he couldn't see who his attackers were. The only thing he knew was that there was more than one of them, and if his backup didn't get to him soon, he'd be a dead man.

Six months later and Elijah still didn't remember what happened between initially being attacked and waking up in the ICU a week later on life support. But he'd always carried the fuzzy image of Camden with a single tear down his cheek.

The sadness that registered in Camden's eyes lit a fire somewhere in Elijah's addled brain that told him there was something, someone worth fighting for. When Elijah had finally awoken, and the only faces he saw were those of his family members, he'd concluded it was just his imagination.

Elijah gently shook himself free of the haunting image. Elijah moved up the steps with the suitcase in hand and stepped inside of the kitchen. He glimpsed his family and Camden sitting at the kitchen table laughing loudly and thought to himself, *Maybe it wasn't a dream at all.*

Chapter Twelve

CAMDEN sat in the living room flanked by the entire Stephenson clan. He made himself comfortable in the oversized armchair, his back straight, one leg crossed over the other, and his hands neatly sitting atop his thigh as he took in Elijah's family.

They were loud, fun, and connected in ways Camden had never experienced on a personal level. Sure, he understood the fundamentals of how a family was supposed to work, but the reality often differed from the ideal.

He'd always thought of himself as fortunate being born into the Warren clan. His family possessed generational wealth that afforded Camden and his parents a luxurious life most couldn't conceive of.

The Warrens never had to worry about having money; they only ever had to worry about using it to their advantage.

And they did.

Ivy League educations, several beautiful homes across the globe, traveling by private accommodations, experiencing the best of what life and the world offered, there were no worries.

Well, not of the financial kind. Instead, his family worried about how to compound their wealth and the prestige it brought them. In the Warren family, you married to improve your fortune, your standing in the community, or both.

It was reminiscent of the intermarriage that took place among European royalty. To preserve the line, they arranged marriages between unwed children.

The Warrens weren't royalty. However, they sought many of the tenets of royalty: wealth, power, and prestige.

But here Camden sat in a room full of laughing people who had no monetary fortunes to speak of, none that he could tell anyway, and they seemed to possess something Camden didn't remember ever witnessing in his own family: happiness.

They were at ease with one another. Invading one another's personal space, finding humor in one another, enjoying one another's company. This was something he'd never experienced in his family.

The laughter died down, and the focus of the conversation shifted as everyone's gaze fell on him.

"So where are you and your family from, Camden?"

Camden blinked for a moment while he pondered how to answer Evelyn Stephenson's question. Elijah must have seen his hesitance and moved closer to him, sitting

on the arm of his armchair and placing a comforting arm around the back of the chair.

A brief nod from Elijah, and Camden smiled at the man and then his mother before speaking.

"Albany."

"Albany?" Evelyn's brown eyes crinkled at the edges with curiosity. "How did you end up all the way down in the five boroughs?"

On paper, his trek from the ideal world of the quiet suburb just outside of the city limits of New York's capital to the faster-paced five boroughs of what New Yorkers considered Downstate seemed odd. However, when your father had your career path planned out from birth, it didn't seem all that strange.

"Work." His answer was a more stripped-down version of the truth, but still the truth. "There was a position in a notable Brooklyn law office available." Camden didn't often disclose what kind of law he practiced or that he was a prosecutor. Sure, it was misleading, but in this case a little misdirection was certainly warranted. "It was far from home, but it was an opportunity I couldn't say no to."

"Couldn't" being the operative word in that sentence. His father's dream of Camden becoming a political powerhouse required Camden's career to be firmly planted in New York's political scene. It didn't matter that Camden would've much preferred to work as a defense attorney. Being a tough-on-crime prosecutor would look better on Camden's résumé.

The work hadn't been terrible. Camden had made lasting acquaintanceships in the DA's office that had made the job bearable. But doing a thing because you were good at it or because someone told you to do it wasn't the same as loving your job.

"So how did you two meet?" This time the question came from Elijah's sister-in-law, Vivienne. She was tempered compared to the rest of the Stephenson family, her eyes bright and her smile easy, lulling Camden into her question.

"Through my boss." Drawing from Elijah's edict that the best lies were rooted in truth, Camden answered easily. "Elijah and my boss are work friends, I guess you'd say. She knew we were both single and suggested we might enjoy getting to know each other."

"That'll make for an interesting story to tell your future children."

Camden thanked the heavens he hadn't been drinking anything. If he had, it would have come spewing out of his mouth. Instead, he stared openly at Evelyn, trying to make certain he'd heard her correctly. The generous smile she wore confirmed Camden hadn't imagined what she'd said.

He had nothing, absolutely nothing, to counter that assumption that he and Elijah would someday have children. He pulled his gaze to Elijah's, hoping he'd know how to better deal with his mother. Dealing with his own parents all these years had been Camden's greatest failure. He wasn't about to manage someone else's.

"Mama!" The stern way Elijah called to her made the older woman grin even wider. "On that note, I think it's time we call it a night. Camden's had a pretty hectic couple of days, and I'm sure he could use some rest."

"Same sleeping arrangements as always, or you want Viv and me to take your room and share the upstairs with the 'rents?"

Camden waited for Elijah's answer to Emmanuel's question. As far as Camden could recall, there were only two bedrooms in this house. The master and the guest room Elijah had placed Camden in earlier. What other sleeping arrangements could Emmanuel be speaking of?

"Nah, you and Viv can keep the room in the basement. Camden and I are in my master. Pops and Mama can take the guest room down the hall once I've made it up."

Camden swallowed his building anxiety. The quick hand job in his basement gym was one thing, but spending a night in the same bed as Elijah was a temptation Camden didn't think wise. They hadn't processed what had happened between them yet. Being locked in the same bed couldn't help their situation.

Elijah stood up, hugged his father and brother, and gave his mother and sister-in-law each a peck on the cheek before he turned his gaze to Camden and extended a hand for Camden to take.

Camden watched his hand for probably what seemed longer than necessary to the rest of the room. Not that he didn't understand the reason Elijah was doing it. No, he understood, but it still somehow seemed so out of character for the way the big man communicated with Camden.

"Camden, you coming?"

Camden blinked a few more times, clearing the fuzz from his head and finally stepping into his role as smitten lover. "I'm sorry," he offered. "I guess I'm more tired than I realized."

He gave one hand to Elijah and used the other to wave good night to Elijah's family. He kept his mouth shut and his face free of the panic growing inside until he stepped into Elijah's room.

Camden looked around the spacious room, hoping to find some sort of sofa for him to sleep on. Although the room was spacious, it wasn't a suite built with separate rooms. There was a large king-sized bed in the middle of the room, two doors—one of which Camden assumed was a bathroom, and the other a closet—and a dresser and chest against two connecting walls.

"So, I guess I'm sleeping on the floor, then?"

Elijah closed the door behind Camden and shrugged his shoulders. "You can if you want to, but I'm too grown to be sleeping on the floor. It's a king-sized bed. There's more than enough room for the two of us."

Elijah disappeared for a few moments behind one door, and Camden heard water running in the shower. When Elijah returned, he was shirtless, with a towel wrapped around his waist.

Camden's mouth went dry, and his heart rate increased by more than a few beats a minute.

Holy hell!

Camden remembered how remarkable Elijah's body had been. He remembered every plane beneath his lips and fingers and how touching him made Camden senseless with need. Seeing him now, still carved with rigid lines of muscle definition, made him thirsty in ways no drink of water would ever quench.

"Not long before my family arrived, we had each other's dicks in our hands. I don't think sleeping in the same bed together should pose an issue. You feel me?"

Camden swallowed hard, trying to pull his dry, thick tongue from the roof of his mouth. It took a few attempts, but he could finally shake the fog from his brain and the dust from his tongue to form a sentence.

"Yes." Camden's voice cracked on the one syllable. He cleared his throat and tried to speak again. "It should be fine."

Elijah shrugged a shoulder as he turned around to return to the bathroom. The high and tight curve of his ass was still visible under the towel hanging precariously off his hips, making Camden's hand itch with the need to grab a handful.

When Elijah disappeared into the bathroom again and Camden heard the audible click of the closed door, he released the breath he hadn't realized he'd been holding and readjusted the growing bulge in the front of his pants.

"This will most definitely not be fine."

Chapter Thirteen

CAMDEN woke to delicious heat plastered to his back and a heavy weight draped over his leg and hip. As his sleepy brain climbed into wakefulness, he realized he should probably be alarmed by whatever it was that had his body almost completely encased. Before he could stir enough concern to muster up panic, a slow smile spread across his lips. He'd slept in Elijah's bed last night.

It hadn't been as glorious as the first time, where desire had woken them both throughout the night to indulge in desperate touches that led to soul-satisfying orgasms. But waking to Elijah's heat, to the hard press of his morning hard-on positioned perfectly in the center of Camden's crease, it was everything he wished he'd sampled in their past.

Elijah's hand spread over Camden's abdomen, sparking a flutter of nerves beneath his touch. Camden remained as still as he could, afraid that waking Elijah would either—A—make him stop touching Camden or—B—continue with what Camden prayed would be the natural progression of this moment, allowing Camden to give into his dangerous need for Elijah.

Elijah's hand slipped downward until it was resting over Camden's straining erection. Elijah's body pressed closer against Camden's back while his hand cupped Camden's cock and balls. The dual actions made Camden burn from the inside out with need.

His muscles ached from being locked in the same position. His hips begged to thrust up into Elijah's hand, to encourage him to do more than just encase his cock with still heat. But Camden couldn't. He knew that if he did, it would end, and this unguarded moment of connection and simple pleasure would be over.

When Elijah tightened his grip on Camden's cock, Camden lost the battle and gave in to the deep moan that rattled up his hollow chest and spilled out into the air.

The second the sound escaped his lips, Elijah's entire body tightened against him, including the hand currently pressed against his cock.

"Shit, Camden." Elijah pulled his hand away from Camden's cock. "I'm sorry."

Camden turned around and whispered, "I'm not." He could feel the nervous smile on his lips as his gaze sought Elijah's. "Please don't stop on my account."

Hunger sparked in Elijah's eyes. Camden could see the internal battle waging inside Elijah at this moment. It was a reasonable reaction. They weren't together under normal circumstances. Camden was a job to Elijah.

Camden had made certain there was nothing more
between them when he left. Indulging in this connection
they seemed to share was going to bring them closer or
rip them apart. Weighing both sides equally, Camden
couldn't tell which scenario was worse. He only knew
what his body was begging for, and common sense be
damned, it wanted Elijah's body plastered all over his.

"Camden, my family is here, and I'm assigned
as your protection detail." Elijah's eyes were soft and
pleading, silently begging Camden to be the adult in the
room. "If this goes south, I could lose my badge. I've just
gotten back on the job. I don't want to risk it."

Camden heard the period on the end of Elijah's
sentence, but in his head and his heart he heard the
"on you" attached firmly before the completion of that
thought.

Well, there goes a lovely start to a Saturday morning.

Camden sat up and pulled himself from the
bed. "I suppose if you're not going to finish what
you started"—he pointed to the tented crotch of his
borrowed sweats—"I may as well tend to it myself."
He straightened his shoulders, his pride refusing to let
Elijah see how much he needed him right now. He may
not be worth the risk, but he'd be damned if he'd let
Elijah know that.

Camden had spent many years pretending. He
pretended to want the life his parents planned for
him. He pretended to not feel smothered by all the
stipulations that life came with. He could also pretend
Elijah's rejection of him didn't sting.

AT the sound of the bathroom door closing shut,
Elijah slammed his fist into a nearby pillow. Camden

should mean nothing to him, nothing more than any other charge placed in his care. This wasn't his first protection detail. He'd never fucked around with someone connected to his job. If his inability to keep his hands to himself caused something to happen to Camden, he'd have a hell of a time explaining to Captain Searlington he was too busy getting his dick wet to notice something was wrong.

He'd done the right thing in turning Camden away. It might have annoyed Camden. Hell, the throbbing cock pushing at his boxer briefs didn't like it either. But he was here to do a job and Camden's safety had to come first.

His safety? Really, Elijah? That's the lie we're going with this morning?

Elijah couldn't entertain the truths his subconscious was trying to shove in his face. To think about any other reason than the job might give Elijah license to reach for what was being offered.

And would that be so bad?

It would be more than bad. It would be a disaster.

Elijah fought to free himself of the feel of Camden's body on his for the first time in five years. He battled to make his body stop waking up in the throes of withdrawal from Camden's touch. It was a sickness, an addiction he didn't want to fall prey to again. He'd kicked the habit cold turkey. To go back now, after being clean for five years, that would be lunacy. Except, last night he'd slipped.

Last night, he'd savored the taste of Camden's mouth. He'd reveled in the skill of the man's touch. He'd lost himself in the desire that threatened to consume him. There was no logical explanation for how he'd let himself do something as reckless as getting his rocks off with the attempted murder victim Elijah was assigned to protect.

If the taste of Camden's lips and the feel of his flesh hot against Elijah's could make him do something so out of character, what might this need he harbored for the man make Elijah do if he gave in to desire fully? If he indulged again, Elijah wasn't so certain he could pull himself away.

Losing control wasn't an option for Elijah. He'd lost control of the situation when he'd been jumped inside that illegal gambling hole. He'd nearly lost his life because of it. Elijah had gone over what little memory he had leading up to the incident countless times. As far as he could see on paper, everything had gone according to plan until two unknowns had stumbled into their gun buy. He should've called it off then. But they'd been working that case for more than six months. They had the leader of a gun trafficking ring in their grasps. If Elijah called off the buy, there was no telling how long it would take to get all the players and parts together again. He should've known it wasn't safe. And like most people who do dumb shit they shouldn't in the heat of the moment, Elijah paid the price.

When Elijah heard the flowing water in the shower stop, he turned his head toward the door and thought of Camden. What would become of Elijah if he lost himself to Camden's control? What would become of them both? Elijah closed his eyes and took a long, deep breath and released it slowly. He'd nearly gotten himself killed. Elijah would be damned if he risked Camden's life the same way.

His burner phone began to slide across his nightstand. Elijah laughed. Why wouldn't his boss pick this exact moment, when his dick was hard and his professional guilt was through the roof, to check in?

"Morning," he choked out. The gruff sound of his voice was still filled with desire and disappointment at the loss of Camden's heat next to him. He cleared his throat, hoping his boss thought sleep was the reason for the rough timbre of his voice.

"You up yet?"

"Yeah. A few minutes now. Any news? We making moves today?"

Elijah looked down at his straining length and shook his head at how fucked-up this entire situation was becoming.

"No. So far Edwards and his people haven't made any new moves. We've been keeping pretty close tabs on them since you left. My man on the inside says nothing's changed. They're still looking for Warren, but most of them think Edwards is just being paranoid by keeping up the search at this point."

Elijah allowed a small bit of relief to course through his system. They weren't in the clear, but if the Path was still sniffing around in Brooklyn, Camden would be fine.

"Everything's as it should be on our end. What about yours? Anything you need to tell me?" Captain Searlington's question made his breath catch in his throat.

Oh, there was a lot he probably should tell her, but either stupidity, selfishness, or pride was keeping him from opening his mouth. While he tried to think up a reply, Elijah heard another voice in the background from Captain Searlington's end.

"Shit!"

"Captain?" Elijah could hear the muffled sounds of the captain's voice as if she were covering the phone with her hand. He called her name again, and suddenly the line was clear, and he could decipher her words again.

"I had Cyber monitoring Warren's electronics and digital accounts. Someone has been accessing his accounts remotely. We just can't narrow down from where. If you were here, I'd be yelling at you for this shit."

If he was there, she'd be yelling at him for much more than this. "It's not him, Cap. He's been on a blackout here. No phones, no electronics whatsoever. Can you tell if they found anything?"

"Not yet. Edwards is a relentless son of a bitch. He's days away from the trial resuming, and he's still got his war dogs scouring for Warren. Just make sure that entitled asshole you got as a roomie keeps his ass off the web. Edwards is desperate. He's trying his damnedest to tie up loose ends."

Chapter Fourteen

"**ALL** right, all right, all right!"

Camden pulled his eyes away from the Sunday newspaper he was reading and looked around for whatever was disturbing the few moments of quiet he had before the Stephenson clan converged on the kitchen. Since Elijah forbade him from scouring the internet for any bit of information about the Path, Camden's only sources of information on the outside world were the paper Elijah's father brought in after his early morning walk, and the television. He'd spent all day yesterday lying on the couch watching television to avoid Elijah and his family. After Elijah's rejection of him, Camden didn't feel all that social. He decided reading might be a better, safer solution to his current state of boredom instead.

To avoid further damage to his ego, Camden made certain he went to bed before Elijah, and was showered and out of the room before he rose. It was a coward's move, but God help him, he didn't think he could swallow that kind of bitter rejection again. After yesterday morning's fiasco, it was best if his mind and his dick were nowhere near Elijah Stephenson.

But are you really avoiding awkward moments with him, though?

It was hard to avoid someone when you couldn't actually leave the house. But Camden would take his solace where he could, and sitting in this kitchen, sipping on his coffee while reading the newspaper was one of the precious few ways he had of removing himself from an embarrassing situation that only threatened to get worse every time he found himself tangled up in Elijah's sheets.

Camden shook his head, refusing to let the thought of how warm and tantalizing the feel of Elijah's body was against his take root. Instead, he focused on the loud smack of Emmanuel's hand on the table.

Camden took another sip of his coffee and bristled. His taste buds still attempting to acclimate to the heaviness of the half-and-half in his morning beverage, he placed his coffee mug on the table, then folded the paper and focused on Emmanuel.

"Did you need something, Emmanuel?"

Elijah's younger brother had a wide grin drawn across his face, coupled with a twinkling of excitement in his eyes. "Yeah, it's Sunday. In the Stephenson household, when we're all together on a Sunday, we play Spades. Why don't you go on upstairs and get my brother so he can make us breakfast while the rest of us get this game started?"

Camden took a moment to look around before he leveled his gaze back at Emmanuel. "I see no one else here. Perhaps it's still a bit too early for cards."

Emmanuel leaned back in his chair and shook his head. "Nah." The casual familiarity of his voice made Camden smile. This man had no clue who Camden was, but inside his brother's home, he was comfortable and apparently had no intentions of letting Camden's surprise appearance change that. "I heard Pops come in from his morning walk about twenty minutes ago. By my calculation, he and Mama should be down here in another ten minutes. My wife will follow close behind. My brother is the only holdout. I suspect you're the reason he's not lurking the halls at the crack of dawn anymore."

Camden lifted a brow and let Emmanuel's thoughts travel wherever he wanted them to without interruption or clarification from Camden. Too bad the reality was nowhere near as sordid as Emmanuel's assumptions. If it was, there'd be no way in hell Camden would be up at this ungodly hour reading a paper, just to get out of Elijah's way. No, he'd be snuggled next to the warm expanse of smooth, strong man he'd left upstairs.

"Well, since it's your family tradition, I believe the responsibility falls to you to summon your brother?"

"You obviously don't have siblings, Camden. No grown-ass man walks into the bedroom his brother has shared with a lover the night before. E and I are cool, tighter than any two brothers could be. But he ain't trying to witness the aftermath of me banging all night, and neither am I." Emmanuel folded his arms across his chest to punctuate his position on the matter. He wasn't going. Camden let a tiny smile slip through. If only

Emmanuel knew he had nothing to fear by walking into Elijah's room.

Camden stood and quickly made his way up the stairs. He stopped, his instinct to knock on the door before he walked in. But then he suspected it would look strange for a man who was supposed to be Elijah's lover to knock before entering the man's bedroom.

He opened the door and stepped inside, closing the door behind him quickly. "Elijah, your brother—" Camden turned, not the least bit prepared for the vision before him: Elijah standing at the foot of the bed, naked, with a towel draped over his shoulder.

The instant dryness in his mouth forced Camden to swallow against the lump sitting at the bottom of his throat. Strong shoulders and arms coupled with perfectly carved muscles on his entire frame made Camden's fingertips itch with need. The deep hue of smooth skin glistened from whatever moisturizer Elijah had previously applied. Camden closed his fists to keep from reaching out for a touch.

"My brother what?"

Camden heard the question, yet his brain couldn't divert enough of his focus to form an answer. Why would it? When you stumbled upon such astonishing beauty, how could you think about trivial things like connecting words to impart meaning?

"Camden? You were about to say something about my brother? Is he being an asshole again?"

Elijah turned around, walking into his closet, gifting Camden with a perfect view of his toned ass before he disappeared inside. Camden used the moment to shake himself free of Elijah's spell. It was obvious Elijah knew he was a walking wet dream. But knowing and expecting the man you've already told you're not interested in to ogle you like a piece of meat was a different story.

When Elijah returned, he was thankfully covered in another pair of his favored sweatpants. The soft fabric hid enough of Elijah's muscular form that Camden could at least form a coherent thought again.

"No, I mean, well, he is your brother." Camden's awkward response seemed to make Elijah smile. "It's my observation he's probably made a career out of being an asshole."

Elijah pointed a finger at Camden as he said, "Hey, lay off my brother, man." Camden might have believed he was serious if it wasn't for the sincere smile pulling at Elijah's full lips. "What's Manny up to?"

"Your brother sent me to fetch you for a game of Spades."

"Shit." Elijah looked at his watch and quickly pulled the T-shirt he held in his hands over his head.

"I told Emmanuel I didn't think you'd appreciate being woken this early for a card game."

"Early?" The frown creasing Elijah's brow made concern swell inside Camden. "Dude, it's never too early for Spades."

Elijah walked past Camden, his quick steps bringing him to the door in no time. "You're really rushing downstairs to play a card game with your family?"

Elijah ran his fingers quickly through his locs before leveling a look mixed with equal parts frustration and disbelief. "Camden, Spades is not just a card game. Friendships and families have been destroyed by this game. For generations, my family has played this game. It's a rite of passage. If you can't play, you can't be part of the clan."

A hearty laugh rose out of Camden's chest. He was certain Elijah would join him. He had to be joking. It was a card game, a popular one if he remembered correctly from his days in a frat house. But loss of friendship and family? Elijah couldn't really mean that.

"Camden." Elijah's voice dropped to that "I'm not to be fucked with" tone. If the terse lines around the perimeter of his square jaw were any indication, Elijah was very serious. "We do not play when it comes to Spades."

"Really?"

Elijah nodded. "Really," he uttered before looking over his shoulder toward the door. "Was Viv up yet? If she sleeps in, maybe I could get in a game or two before she gets up."

Lost on Elijah's train of thought, Camden raised his hand before asking his question. "I know there's probably a logical explanation why you're concerned about Vivienne being up, but I don't understand why you can't play if she's awake."

"It's a partners game. She and Manny team up against my parents all the time. The only time I get to play is as a substitute for one. I mean, I play with my boys on the job every now and again. But believe me, there's nothing like a game of Spades with the Stephensons."

Camden's curiosity was piqued. He'd spent all of yesterday in the presence of Elijah's family, and he could testify that most things he'd witnessed the Stephensons do was unlike any other family, certainly not Camden's, anyway. Who else welcomed a total stranger into the fold the way Evelyn had with no proper vetting? Who else would make Camden feel so welcome without testing his worth, what he could bring to the table?

Uncertain of what he was about to encounter, Camden fell into step behind Elijah as they made their way down the stairs. He might not know what Spades with the Stephensons was like, but the idea of spending time with the Stephensons doing anything brought an unfamiliar excitement Camden didn't quite understand, and honestly, he had no intention of trying to explore it either. For once, he would not look at the angles of the situation. He was just going to enjoy it.

Chapter Fifteen

"YOU sure you wanna do this, brother?"

Elijah was asking himself that exact question. Only, he refused to let his younger brother know it. Emmanuel was cocky enough that Elijah didn't need to add to his ego.

Elijah leveled a concerned glance at Camden sitting across the table from him. In pure Camden fashion he sat painfully straight in his chair with perfect posture. His shoulders squared, he winked an eye at Elijah and blew him a kiss across the table. He was unconcerned, unbothered in a way that both enticed and frightened Elijah.

Spades was not a game of chance. It was skill, all skill. It was also highly competitive. Add his family to the mix, and there was a real possibility there would be spilled blood somewhere on his kitchen floor.

"Camden, are you certain about this? If you can't play, just back away now."

Camden let his gaze move around the expanse of the table, carefully assessing Emmanuel, Vivienne, and then Elijah. The aloofness Elijah found in his eyes made his stomach turn. He didn't get it. Camden didn't understand how serious this game was. Which meant one thing, Elijah would have to listen to his already annoying brother brag about his and Vivienne's impending win.

Elijah's chest tightened when he noticed something different about Camden. It wasn't a noticeable change, something only a person who carefully studied the man up close would recognize. In the depths of those crystal blue eyes, there was certainty.

Elijah remembered that look. The moment Camden had arrived for their date. As soon as he locked eyes with him, Elijah could see Camden was certain in their connection. He never wavered, never relented. Until the wee hours of the morning, he showed Elijah what it meant to have a lover who could play your body like an instrument. A lover whose talent was amplified because there were no questions, no hesitations, just simple confidence and the unimaginable pleasure it brought.

Elijah nodded his head and sat back against his chair, calmer than he had been and resigned that Camden had this. He didn't know why. Nothing about Camden said he'd spent any real time entrenched in this time-honored card game, but Camden's sense of calm made Elijah feel at ease.

"Y'all in or you out?" Emmanuel demanded as he shuffled the cards. His lips curved into a smile as he watched Camden's lips do the same. They were more than in, they came to play.

"Deal the cards, Manny. We got this."

"Oh, so you think you can take Viv and me since the pretty boy showed up? Come on, big brother, let me spank that ass again. Ya man ain't got no game for us. How many books you got?"

Elijah looked down at his cards and counted the expected hands he thought he could win. With a king of clubs, an ace of hearts, and the coveted ace of spades, he was certain he had at least four books won.

"I got four. How many books you got, Cam?"

He watched Camden study his hand. His confidence in Camden's playing ability waned just slightly as the man slowly examined his cards.

"Books?"

That confused look Camden offered made Elijah's stomach twist in knots. "Books are the hands won in each play."

"Oh, you mean tricks?"

Relief spread through Elijah. *Okay, maybe this was just a case of things being lost in translation.*

"Tricks?" Manny's response made Elijah cut his eyes at his brother across the table. "That might be the technical term, but when us melanated folk play, we call 'em books."

"Ignore him, Camden. How many do you have?"

"Five."

Elijah wasn't a cautious bidder, but for someone he assumed wasn't an avid player of Spades, five books in the first hand seemed a little too much.

"You sure you got five? Maybe you want to take another look before you decide?"

Camden shook his head. "I'm certain. I can win five tricks."

Elijah took a deep breath and tried to calm his nerves. It was only the first hand. They usually played five or six in a set. If Camden fucked up now, Elijah still had time to pull them out later.

"All right, Vivienne." Elijah gave a nod to his sister-in-law, who sat with a pencil hovering over the notepad sitting in front her. "Put us down for nine books." She scribbled their bid next to their names, and then wrote a four next to hers and his brother's.

Elijah threw down the ace of hearts. His strategy was to win as many as he could up front and then focus on helping Camden make his bids. When Vivienne threw down the three of hearts, Elijah chewed the inside of his lip as he waited for Camden to throw down a card.

Elijah had the highest card in the suit. The only trump to that was if someone broke the first spade.

Just let me have this hand, Camden. You better not cut me.

Camden put down a four of hearts, followed by Emmanuel's eight of hearts. The book was Elijah's.

Elijah breathed a sigh of relief and his skin prickled as he caught the sultry smile Camden leveled at him. That smile said everything Elijah needed to hear from Camden.

I've got your back. You can depend on me. You can trust me.

A shiver slid down Elijah's back. This kind of support from anyone other than his family or his fellow officers was odd. He expected support in those relationships; they were obligatory situations. This felt different, freely offered. And as wrong as Elijah knew it was to accept, the lonely part of him that was always around the group, but never part of it, danced a happy two-step.

Camden continued to follow Elijah's lead throughout the game, catching the silent signals he threw without alerting his brother and sister-in-law. The fact that they could communicate without actually speaking, that they for once weren't getting their signals crossed, made his heart leap with excitement, sobering him in ways Elijah couldn't explain. It was a card game. Something done to pass the time. And yet, sitting across the table from this man, watching him match Elijah play for play, bound him tighter to Camden than he'd ever been with another human being.

It was strange, but Elijah didn't have time to question it. He was too busy winning books and pissing his brother off to care about why having a partner who could read you when no one else could made happiness flutter in the most secret places of his soul.

"Dammit, Viv." Emmanuel slammed his hand down against the table, the vibration of his frustration and anger making Elijah smile. "I know you saw that damn queen of diamonds I threw out. How you gonna cut me with an ace of diamonds? What kind of bullshit is that?"

"Don't come for me, Manny." The narrowed slits of his sister-in-law's eyes made Elijah chuckle. Vivienne was the coolest, calmest person he knew. She'd have to be to deal with his hyper-ass brother. But when she was angry, she could cut you with just a look from across the room. "That was all I had."

The nervous way Emmanuel swallowed made Elijah's chuckle evolve into a loud roll of laughter. The low growl slipping between the flat line of Emmanuel's lips told Elijah his laughter was making his brother's obviously bad mood worse.

Fuck him! It's no worse than I've suffered from his relentless taunting over the years.

Emmanuel clicked his tongue and waited for Vivienne to start the next hand. When it was his turn to play, he snatched his next card out of his hand and slammed it on the table. Before he could pull his hand back, Camden shook his head at Emmanuel.

"Excuse me, younger Mr. Stephenson. I think we have a problem here."

"The only problem we have is that you and my brother are fucking up my good mood."

Camden shook his head and smiled playfully. "Now, Emmanuel, I think we both know you're not being completely honest. I distinctly remember you throwing out a low spade early to beat Elijah's ace of clubs. A few hands later, and you're throwing out a ten of clubs to beat everyone else's low-ranking cards in the suit. If I remember correctly, isn't the term for that 'reneging'?"

"You calling me a cheater, newbie?"

Elijah threw a pretzel at his brother, popping Emmanuel in his temple. "No, I am. Turn over your damn books and let's have a look."

Emmanuel paused for a minute, probably trying to think of a way to get out of his current predicament. His hesitation in and of itself was a clue that his brother's history of cheating when he was losing was repeating itself.

Emmanuel finally turned his books face up, and they all saw that Camden's observation was accurate.

"You's a cheating-ass bastard, Manny." Elijah's statement was met with Emmanuel's middle finger pointing straight in the air as a reply.

"You just mad because you can't play. Stop being a hater, Elijah."

They'd been having this same argument since they were kids sitting at the table playing with their parents. And although Emmanuel was still the same annoying little opportunist he was when they were kids, sitting here having this familiar conversation in front of Camden soothed him. As if a missing piece to his usual routine had miraculously appeared.

This was usually the part where things escalated to one of them flipping tables in the game. But instead of his anger rising, contentment spread through him. He faced Camden, reached over the table, and offered him a hand. When Camden accepted it, Elijah slapped his palm against Camden's in camaraderie and nodded his head.

"Good eye."

Elijah leaned back in his chair, the muscles in his mouth trying hard to stave off the smile blooming across his lips. It was just a silly game they were playing. How could it make him feel so tethered to the man sitting across from him, smiling openly, making the cold dark spaces of Elijah's soul feel warmth for the first time in a long while?

Yeah, it was only a game. Elijah had to remember that none of this was real. However, when his suspicion and disbelief tried to horn their way in on the good time he was having, Elijah's smile burgeoned until he couldn't hide it any longer. And if he was completely honest, he had no desire to hide how happy he was in that moment.

Chapter Sixteen

ELIJAH turned on the hot water at his double-basin kitchen sink. A few squirts of dish detergent, and the dirty dishes were quickly swallowed by a mountain of suds.

He was still sailing on his Spades win against his brother, and then later his parents. Never in his history of family tournaments had Elijah fared so well. He glanced to his right and found Camden standing near the table, smiling in Elijah's direction.

"I take it you're still happy about beating your brother?"

That was an understatement. Spending all these years as a substitute for any of the major players because he didn't have a partner cut Elijah in ways he'd never been able to voice. However, spending the day playing with Camden as his backup gave Elijah a sense of pride he'd never thought he'd experience outside of work.

"It's never a bad time when I get to shut my brother down." Elijah returned his attention to the sink just in time to keep the water from spilling over the sides. "Thanks for the help with the game. I gotta admit I never thought you'd be able to play like that. Where'd you learn?"

"In college." His answer sounded final, as if there was nothing left to share. No story to help understand. After the way they'd connected playing cards with his family all day, Elijah assumed Camden would show him a little more of himself. He began to give in to the idea that perhaps he was wrong until Camden said, "My roommate in college wasn't part of the trust fund club, so many of our classmates didn't exactly jump over themselves to reach out and make him feel welcome. I invited him to a poker tournament to kind of break the ice, but he couldn't play. I taught him; he played and made a little pocket money. A week later, he'd invited friends over, and they played Spades. Noticing my fascination with the game, he taught me."

Elijah was thankful to whoever that roommate was. The day spent playing had done more than give Elijah a chance to beat his brother, or even bond with his family. It had given him the chance to see a little sliver of the real Camden.

"You had a good teacher."

Camden nodded his head while emptying the rest of the dishes still sitting on the table. A sight that should have seemed foreign to Elijah, but the spark of fire igniting in his belly as he watched the man do something as simple as scrape dirty dishes in his kitchen was more than right. It was natural. As if it should happen every night after a shared meal between them.

"Need help?"

Elijah turned his head to watch Camden bringing the discarded dishes from the table to the sink. He raised a skeptical brow at Camden's offer. "You wash dishes?"

Camden added the pile of dishes to the already halfway-full sink and sighed. "I'm uncertain if it's a task that requires that much skill. Soapy water and a scrubbing brush usually do the trick." Again, Elijah warmed at the thought of Camden in his home doing simple domestic things with him. Why the idea of sharing something so mundane with Camden made his fingers itch to pull him in and hold him close, Elijah didn't know. "If you have gloves, that would be great." Camden displayed his neatly trimmed fingernails, giving them a serious, assessing look. "Suds are hell on a manicure."

Elijah shook his head and gazed up at the ceiling for a few moments. There was the real Camden: proper, prissy, and too damn delicate to work with his hands. Elijah dried his wet hands on the towel, hung it over his shoulder, and moved out of Camden's way. "I wasn't asking if you knew how. I was asking if you did. It's hard to believe a pampered preppy like you would know anything about picking up after himself. You don't have a maid?"

Elijah saw the smile on Camden's face, and relief spread through him. He wasn't trying to offend him. He was genuinely curious about Camden's background. Right now, all he had to work on were his assumptions.

"If I still lived at either of my parents' homes, then yes, there is a full house staff at my disposal. But I live in a one-bedroom in Brooklyn Heights. There's not enough space for a live-in maid. I have a cleaning lady who comes in once a week to keep the place tidy, but the day-to-day cleaning of it falls on my shoulders."

Camden's smile faltered a little as he stole a quick glance at him. "You think so little of me, Elijah. Don't you? I mean, as a human being."

Elijah took the freshly scrubbed dish Camden handed him and dried it with a nearby towel. "I don't know you, Camden. You never gave me the chance."

Elijah could see the bob of Camden's Adam's apple and wondered if his statement was too blunt. It was the truth. Camden had disappeared from Elijah's life after one amazing night together. The only things he knew about Camden were the intimate details about his lovemaking, but nothing more.

Elijah knew how sensitive the skin was at the base of Camden's neck. Every time Elijah touched it, Camden would shiver with need. Elijah knew how much Camden enjoyed having the underside of his balls licked. He'd damn near lost his load when Elijah traced his tongue across them, begging for Elijah not to stop. He knew Camden loved facing his partner during sex whether he was being fucked or doing the fucking. Any position that would allow him to kiss his lover senseless always increased his enjoyment. He knew Camden didn't believe the false narrative that a strong man like Elijah wouldn't enjoy being bent over and fucked relentlessly. That, paired with the fact that Camden liked giving as much as he did receiving had made their one night unforgettable.

He knew so many intimate things about Camden. Had savored learning every single one of them too. But he knew almost nothing about who Camden was on the inside, and what made him tick.

"I suppose running off the way I did didn't leave much opportunity for you to get to know me, did it?"

The man wasn't lying.

Elijah saw tight lines appear around the profile of Camden's jaw and wondered if he was pressing too hard.

"Cam, I didn't mean to upset you."

Camden placed the dirty dish he was holding into the water and turned to Elijah. His eyes were cast down and shoulders drooped just slightly, ruining whatever charm school lesson about perfect posture Elijah was sure someone like Camden would've been taught. In Camden's world, Elijah imagined it was a rule you had to walk around impeccably put together. But here and now, Elijah didn't see something to be scolded over. He saw vulnerability that made him want to scoop Camden up and protect him from everyone, including himself.

"No, I can't get upset with you for telling the truth. The way I left was inexcusable. I owed you better than that."

"I don't know about you owing me anything." Elijah threw his drying towel over his shoulder and faced Camden. "I never understood why you disappeared the way you did. After our date, I thought we connected. The way we were in bed…." He remembered the sensation of being so in sync with another person's body. "I didn't understand what happened. Then I realized you were just slumming, and building something beyond that night wasn't on your agenda."

"It was never about you, Elijah."

Elijah placed the dish he was holding on the counter. Despite Camden's statement, when Elijah had woken up to emptiness and silence that morning, the ache in his ass and his heart informed him otherwise.

Camden grabbed the towel from Elijah's shoulder and dried his hands before speaking again. It was as if the mundane motions gave him an opportunity to build up the nerve to speak his mind.

"Elijah, that night we spent together was more than I ever expected. I wasn't thrilled about my boss setting me up with her friend, but when I met you, I knew she'd put me on the path to finding something irreplaceable."

The word "irreplaceable" made Elijah's heart swell. Camden was a lawyer. A good one according to his record. Choosing the right words to express himself, to make the most impact, was part of what made him so good at his job. Selecting that word was intentional.

"Then what was it about? Because I've never been able to figure it out. Everything about the way you left just made me feel like I wasn't what you wanted or wasn't worth your time."

Camden hung his head as if the shame of his actions was too much for him to overcome. The pose struck Elijah as odd. The word "shame" wasn't something he associated with Camden. But that's exactly the way Camden's body language was reading now.

"My father has planned my life out for me from birth. He has great political aspirations for me. He believes my life and career have to meet certain standards if I'm to be the first openly gay president. The first step is me becoming the district attorney before my fortieth birthday. That position will lead to either a mayoral or gubernatorial run, which will lead to a presidential campaign. But before I run, I need to present the perfect package to the world. I need to settle down with the right man. One who comes from as powerful a political family as I do. One who can model the picture of consistent, wholesome, dedicated love to the masses of politicians and constituents."

Elijah knew what it was to have his mama harping on him about finding a good man. However, this sounded nothing like that. The deep lines appearing around Camden's mouth and his eyes declared this far outweighed a meddling mother.

"His plan has never allowed me to step outside of his outline for my life. Well, not until the one night I shared with you. It was perfect. It was everything I dreamed a night with the right man, a man of my own choosing, could be. But then the morning came, and my father sent me a text telling me he'd set up a meeting with a potential candidate for the role of husband, and I knew everything we'd shared that night would never be possible in my world."

Elijah moved closer to Camden, placing a hand against his cheek, hoping to take away some of the tension that seemed to be building while Camden spoke about his father.

"Camden, it's your life. You don't have to do anything you don't want to."

The loud sigh that slipped through Camden's lips weighed on Elijah. To see Camden, the upbeat, quick-witted man he knew, carrying something so heavy pained Elijah.

"When you're born into the world I am, it's not as simple as finding your own path. Disobedience means exile. And as much as I want freedom, I don't think I could handle exile either."

Camden lifted his eyes, the bright blue sullied with sadness leaving a dull, almost unrecognizable shade in its place. "I desperately wanted more with you, Elijah. What I experienced when we talked, when we laughed, when we made love, it's never left me."

There Camden went again with those deliberate word choices. It hadn't escaped Elijah's notice he'd called their time together in bed "making love." Elijah swallowed the lump of emotion bottled up in his throat. He'd never allowed himself to label the intimacy they'd shared as lovemaking. How could he? To do so would've worsened the blow of being tossed away so easily by someone Elijah connected with on almost a spiritual level.

"Me either." The words fell from Elijah's mouth on a soft breath. So soft he had to wonder if they'd come from him. They were absolute truth, though. He'd never been completely free of that night. It was always somewhere in the back of his mind, haunting his present, reminding him of what he wanted most, but could never have. "I wish you'd brought this to me then. We could've worked it out, Camden."

He shook his head. "You don't think I wanted that? You don't think I wanted to tell you everything and hope you'd take enough pity on me to choose me, choose us anyway? The only thing I could've offered you was a life in the shadows. You deserved better than that."

Elijah shook his head, then stepped closer to Camden. He leaned forward and pressed his forehead to Camden's as he placed a hand at the nape of Camden's neck. "No, Camden. What I deserved was the opportunity to make that decision for myself. And I'm so sorry you didn't trust either of us enough to share this with me back then."

"Why?" Camden's one-word question hung in the air, making it heavy with uncomfortable anticipation.

Elijah pulled Camden into his arms and hugged him to disperse some of the nervous energy Camden's tense body displayed. "Because we could've been awesome together."

Elijah pulled away from the hug and looked into Camden's eyes. He saw a familiar mixture of sadness and regret that Elijah had only witnessed once before.

"You were there, weren't you?"

Camden's confusion was clear in the pinched lines of his brow. "There where? When?"

Elijah kept his gaze leveled at Camden. "My father told me you were at the hospital after my attack. But I keep remembering you standing at my bedside during one of my rare moments of lucidity. You were worried and upset and you kept asking me to fight. I've always thought I was hallucinating. But I wasn't, was I? You really were there?"

Camden didn't answer at first. In fact, his silence stretched out into an awkward gap of nothingness. If this had been one of their prior encounters, Elijah would've filled in the blanks with some smartassed comment. But this moment was too important for that. Not just because of Elijah's need to know, but also because Elijah sensed that this moment could become their turning point if they both dug in and did the work.

Camden returned his gaze to Elijah's. There was none of his usual cockiness there. Camden was always confidence and flair. But tonight, the subdued way his shoulders folded in and his gaze wavered every few seconds revealed the man was lacking the usual dose of self-assurance Camden seemed to exude with great ease.

"I was there." His answer was quiet and small. "I was in a meeting with the DA when the news of your attack arrived. I knew I had no right to be there, but I needed to know you would make it. So, I used my ADA's badge to get me inside your room."

Camden took a deep breath as if the memory of that night was too much for him to bear. It was almost like he needed to fortify himself to be transported back to that time.

Elijah understood that kind of hesitation. He had it every single time his mind or his therapist wanted him to walk back into that black moment. But why would Camden?

"There's no valid reason to explain away my presence in your hospital room. I just knew I had to get to you. Even with so much time passing between us, even knowing you would probably send me away, I still had to be there."

"Why?" Camden lowered his eyes again in response to Elijah's question. Elijah placed a single finger under Camden's chin and lifted until their gazes were level again.

"Because I was afraid you'd die, and I'd never have the chance to tell you how much that one night with you meant."

The longing and regret Elijah saw in Camden's gaze pulled at his heart, making his need to protect Camden sit in the middle of his chest like deadweight. He leaned forward, placing gentle hands on either side of Camden's face, and pressed a soft kiss on the man's mouth.

The kiss was tentative, and part of Elijah hated that. They'd wasted so much time. Five years after their first night together and they were still at the stage where liberties couldn't be taken, where Elijah didn't know for certain that his advances would be welcomed or rejected. But the satisfying moan that seemed to come from somewhere deep inside Camden led Elijah to believe the kiss was something they both desired.

When Elijah tried to pull away, Camden wrapped his arms around his neck and kissed Elijah with fierce intention. The hard press of their lips, the excitement of strong fingers touching him, the satisfying moans of pleasure wafting into the air all reassured Elijah both of them desired this moment.

The heat of anticipation burned through Elijah's system as Camden deepened the kiss. It overran his senses with the taste of Camden's mouth and the feel of his body pressed so closely against his. If they were in this house alone, that wouldn't have been much of a problem. But getting lost in the delicious taste of Camden's tongue wasn't something Elijah could afford with his entire family positioned throughout his house.

With deliberate moves, Elijah gentled their kisses, pulling away from Camden.

"I swear to God, Elijah, if you push me away again, I won't be responsible for what I do."

Elijah smiled, leaning in to place another quick peck on Camden's lips. "I have no intention of pushing you away again. I just don't want my mama to walk in on us ripping each other's clothes off at my kitchen sink."

Camden nodded in agreement. "As much as your mother seems to love me, I don't think she wants to see that, either. Upstairs, then?"

Elijah shook his head. "No, I've got a better idea. Follow me."

Elijah extended his hand to Camden and waited for him to accept it. The moment Camden took to place his palm against Elijah's might have been a source of concern if Elijah hadn't seen blazing desire coupled with resolute decisiveness in Camden's gaze. He wanted Elijah—that much had been true the first night they'd met. But tonight, as Camden intertwined careful fingers with his, Elijah could see in the depths of his eyes that for the first time in five years, he was choosing Elijah.

"Lead the way, Lieutenant."

Chapter Seventeen

CAMDEN held Elijah's hand. Partly to follow Elijah's lead, but mostly because he wanted to hold on to the magic of the moment they'd created in that kitchen.

Camden recognized the spark when Elijah pulled him into his powerful embrace. From the first time he'd encountered Elijah to now, it was there. It was strong, clutching at his heart, stoking a fire Camden had struggled to smother all this time.

Back then, the excitement was about experiencing something new with a man that ticked all of Camden's boxes, all except the one his parents would insist be checked off. But tonight, Camden knew what to expect. He'd relived every moment in his head and heart during their separation. What was new was the hope that this moment could extend itself beyond the satisfaction Camden knew he and Elijah would gift to each other.

A short walk through the mudroom and they were walking through a connecting door into what Camden assumed was a garage. Only after Elijah turned the lights on did Camden see this space wasn't a garage at all. It was fashioned into a one-room studio. A kitchen area in the back and an open space that doubled as both a living room and a bedroom at once.

The space was bathed in tranquil deep blue hues that invited you to sit down and rest for a while. An offer Camden intended to take full advantage of for as long as Elijah allowed.

"When I was working on rebuilding my body in rehab after my attack, my therapist suggested I work on rebuilding my confidence too." The quiet sound of Elijah's voice was small and so fragile, like a delicate, breakable thing that needed the utmost care. Camden's heart raced with concern as he stepped closer to offer his unspoken support. "She told me to find a space I could be safe enough to be weak. I'd thought of renting this space out when I moved in, or even leaving it empty for visiting family members. But the day I got my approval to return to work, I knew I needed to find someplace to be as broken as my mind told me I was."

Elijah must have seen the questions forming on Camden's face, because he held up a single finger to stop him from speaking, and pulled Camden farther inside. He motioned for Camden to take a seat next to him on the large daybed sitting in the center of the room.

"Why did getting your clearance for active duty papers make you feel weak?"

Elijah kept hold of Camden's hand, stroking it before returning his gaze to Camden's face. "There's only been two instances where I've been caught off guard. The first was when I met you. Everything from the way we connected, to the way you took off in the morning left me shocked and uncomfortable. As good as my instincts were, they seemed to be completely wrong about you, and my expectations of what that night would be."

"And the second?" Camden's question met with a weary smile from Elijah. It was a look Camden wasn't familiar with. It made him feel awkward and out of place, as if there was no space for him in whatever moment Elijah seemed to revisit.

"The second was the night of my attack. I'm always meticulous in my job, Camden. I knew all the angles, every single time I walked into a bad situation while undercover. But that night, somehow the tweakers who ended up almost killing me hadn't made me uneasy enough to be on my guard. I thought I could handle them. They were just meth-heads. It wasn't until I woke up in a hospital bed, clinging to a very thin thread, I realized how wrong I was. And from that moment, I had to question if I really knew as much as I thought I did. Was I really the baddest cop on the block?"

Camden sat quietly, not pushing Elijah to say more, but hoping his presence would provide comfort and encourage him to continue sharing his thoughts.

"When you left that night…. It was the first time I questioned my worth. It was the first time I wondered if I wasn't enough. When I got attacked, it was the first time I questioned if I was enough to get the job done."

"Then why take this case, Elijah?"

Elijah shook his head as he turned to face Camden. "My captain assigned me this case. I didn't choose it."

Camden's head dropped, and he pulled away from the warmth they appeared to be creating from the moment they stepped into this place.

Elijah must have noticed Camden's retreat, because he tightened his hold on Camden's hand and tugged him closer.

"I may not have had a choice in taking this case, Camden. But getting to know you over these last few days, figuring out that my radar wasn't as wrong as I believed where you're concerned, helped me in ways I didn't know I needed."

Elijah released Camden's hand, letting his own travel slowly up Camden's arm until his fingers caressed Camden's jaw. The feel of them rubbing back and forth against the thin layer of stubble there made his breath catch in his throat. "I didn't know I hadn't been breathing since that night, holding my breath, waiting for what I was missing." Elijah leaned in, punctuating his sentence with a ghost of a kiss to Camden's angled jaw. The barely there touch made his skin buzz with anticipation of the next touch Elijah would gift him with.

"I didn't know how desperately I wanted to be enough for you, Camden." Elijah snaked his fingers through Camden's hair, his fingernails grazing his scalp, making the skin warm beneath his touch. "When my ego kicked in and told me that your slight was meaningless, that I didn't care anyway, I didn't know there was a reason I was holding on to that night." The tip of Elijah's tongue tickled the curve of his earlobe. The touch was so light and yet his cock instantly responded, plumping up in anticipation of what Camden prayed would follow.

"And I wouldn't have known how amazing it feels to connect with you again." Elijah traced his tongue down the curve of Camden's neck, eliciting a shiver that shook him to his core. Camden had been so busy trying to regain his composure that he hadn't noticed they were now horizontal on the daybed. Elijah settled himself between Camden's legs, leaning on one elbow as he looked down at Camden with a generous smile. "If I hadn't been forced to take this case, I never would've known my instincts were right when they told me how special you were, and how I needed to do everything in my power to keep you near."

Elijah tugged Camden into a deep kiss, their mouths moving in rhythmic harmony as they tasted each other. Elijah pulled away, leaving just enough space for their gazes to meet as they struggled to catch their breath. "I may have had no choice in taking this case, Cam. But I'm protecting you for my selfishness, because I've realized that being without you is too high a price for me to pay."

Something broke inside him at the end of Elijah's declaration. The dam he'd used to suppress this tangible thing that grew inside him for Elijah, rearranging the inner workings of his heart, was also breaking. He'd spent a majority of the last five years living in denial too. He'd told himself Elijah was nothing more than a one-night stand. A meaningless fling that had no place in his life. But lying beneath this man, having the chance to be pulled into the craziness that was the Stephenson family, revealed to Camden just how much he'd lost by walking away from Elijah.

"I want everything we never had the chance to have after that night. If you don't want that too, then you'd better tell me now."

Camden was hiding out in a quiet neighborhood in Westchester from deadly criminals who wanted his head on a platter. His parents, although aware of his current situation, were probably still planning his next political move and his marriage to the right man. But lying on this bed, enveloped in Elijah's warmth and desire, Camden knew he couldn't give one single damn about any of that.

He'd been numb all this time. After experiencing what real emotion was, how the beauty and pain of it were proof of living and not just existing, he couldn't give that up for anyone. Not the Path, not for his parents, not for his father's political aspirations for Camden. No, he wanted all the admissions Elijah offered him, and he was just selfish enough to reach out and take what he wanted this time.

"This won't be as easy as me saying yes, Elijah. This business with the Path wanting me dead might complicate things. And my father will not be exactly happy about me being romantically linked to a blue-collar cop."

Elijah maneuvered himself to the side of Camden and placed a firm kiss on his mouth before locking gazes with him. "This business with the Path will be over in a matter of days. My captain and my team will make sure of that. And as long as we're inside these walls, you're safe. As for your father, I'm not really all that concerned about what makes him happy. As long as you're happy, that's all that matters."

Camden closed his eyes and chuckled before returning his gaze to Elijah's. "You only say that because you've never met my father."

"No, Camden, your father hasn't met me."

The fire that burned inside the depths of his obsidian gaze scorched Camden's fears and filled him with a warmth that called to the deepest parts of his soul. The man had hardly touched him, and his body was so on edge, Camden wasn't certain he could control himself for much longer.

"Elijah, do me a favor?" Elijah narrowed his eyes and nodded his head. "Could we stop talking about my father and the crazy people trying to kill me, so you can fuck me?"

One corner of Elijah's mouth rose in a half smile, making Camden's entire body tingle at the sight. "Oh yes." The playful, decadent tone of Elijah's voice made Camden ache with want. "We can most definitely do that."

Chapter Eighteen

ELIJAH kept that sexy-as-sin half smile on his face as he pulled his gaze down the length of Camden's body. He sat up, then lifted Camden up with him. When Camden tried to sit beside Elijah, he shook his head.

"Nah, that's not your seat."

Camden didn't exactly follow his meaning until he smoothed a large palm over the top of his clothed cock. The gesture was both an invitation and a command, one Camden had no intention of turning away. Eager to fulfill Elijah's request, Camden stripped his shirt off and quickly disposed of his sweatpants and boxer briefs a second later. He figured they'd need to come off soon enough, no sense in wasting time doing it later.

As he straddled Elijah's lap, the spread of his full lips into a broad smile told Camden his assumption was right. Naked Camden was what they both wanted. Now, if Camden could just get Elijah to divest himself of his clothing too so Camden could get to that delicious flesh beneath, everything would be perfect in his world.

Camden reached for the hem of Elijah's T-shirt and was disappointed when Elijah placed his hands on top of Camden's and shook his head. He was about to protest, but then Elijah moved his hands to Camden's flanks, then around his back, until they traveled to his shoulders. Elijah's movements were tender, gentle, and so slow, painstakingly slow—the simple slide of his flesh over Camden's building his need and frustration with little effort. Except for Camden sitting in his lap naked, they'd barely made it to a place where Camden would call this intimate or overtly sexual. But being near Elijah like this, feeling his heat, his desire—it made every touch, every look, every sound seem so arousing, Camden could hardly stand it.

Elijah placed a firm grip at the back of Camden's neck, pulling him forward until their lips met in a hard press. From that moment on, the gentleness Elijah seemed determined to exact on Camden fell away and was replaced by burning desperation. Teeth clicked, tongues tangled as they struggled to taste each other, and Camden's lungs burned from their need to breathe. But when the decision was his next breath or breaking away from the pleasure of Elijah's kiss, he'd gladly suffocate.

Elijah kept one hand pressed against Camden's neck, holding Camden's lips right where he wanted them, while he moved the other to Camden's straining length. The tight fist around his cock, coupled with the stroke of Elijah's thumb across the straining domed cap, forced Camden to take a breath. But when he tried to pull away from Elijah's lips, the firm press of his hand at Camden's neck kept him locked in a torturous kiss.

Camden's hips moved of their own accord as his cock chased the warmth and friction Elijah's closed palm provided. Camden didn't care that Elijah's grip was dry; he didn't care he would probably end up with some kind of abrasion on his cock if he fucked Elijah's hand the way his body desperately needed him to. Thankfully, Elijah had better sense than he did, because he released Camden's cock without warning.

Before Camden could lament the loss of Elijah's hand or the glorious way it gripped his leaking cock, Elijah broke their kiss and moved his mouth to Camden's ear to whisper, "Feed me."

Camden groaned as he closed his eyes and let his head drift back. He shivered at the almost painful weight of his heavy balls while the image of Elijah swallowing his cock whole danced behind his closed lids. "Dammit, Elijah." Camden shifted, restless in Elijah's lap, tugging at his sensitive sac to stave off the orgasm that was already building. "You can't say shit like that and not expect me to lose my load."

The tip of Elijah's tongue caressed his earlobe. The electric sensation sent tiny shocks through his system, making him tremble with need. "I thought the point of this entire exercise was for both of us to lose our loads?"

"It is," Camden answered on a short-whispered breath. "But not like this."

Elijah slipped his hand around the base of Camden's cock again, making it throb, causing Camden to struggle to keep from tipping over the edge.

"How, then?" The quiver in Elijah's voice made Camden open his eyes. He pulled back far enough to lock stares with Elijah to discover blazing desire and burning need.

Camden ran a slow finger across Elijah's lips, delighting at the thought of having them wrapped around him, sucking Camden into oblivion. He shook himself free of the mini fantasy playing out in his head and focused on forming an answer to Elijah's question. "With your cock buried to the hilt inside me."

Elijah pulled Camden in for another kiss, his tongue pushing past Camden's lips, demanding entrance to his mouth, licking and stroking Camden into a desperate frenzy.

"I promise to give you everything you want." He punctuated his sentence with a quick kiss to Camden's lips and a tight squeeze of his hand on Camden's cock. "But please, Cam." Elijah's tongue traced his lips in hungry anticipation as he looked down at the sight of Camden's straining length, running his thumb through the pearl of precum resting on Camden's purplish cap. Elijah smiled just before swirling his captured treasure around the tip, pulling a desperate moan from Camden. "Let me taste that first."

The sheer bliss on Elijah's face as he stroked Camden's cock made the breath catch in the middle of his chest. Elijah, a man who wore his passion on his heart for everyone to see, a man who lived loud and bold in the world, had leveled Camden with a few whispered words and the swipe of his finger.

The press of cushions against his back brought about the realization that Elijah must've moved him off his lap and laid Camden down on the bed. He hadn't a clue when it happened; he was too busy trying to remember to breathe to focus on anything nonessential like how he ended up on his back or when Elijah had stripped—as evidenced by the electric sensation of Elijah's smooth, hot skin pressed against Camden's.

Elijah's fingers were at his hole demanding admittance. He tensed for a moment, but the smooth glide of Elijah's digits inside him eased the anxiousness. He turned his head to the side and saw a bottle of lubricant that Camden couldn't remember seeing before.

Am I that fucking lost that I didn't even see him get it?

Camden didn't have time to dwell on the thought. As Elijah settled between Camden's legs, stroking him from the inside, he swallowed Camden's cock from tip to root. Camden's eyes crossed, and his head pushed deeper into the bed cushions as his back bowed. If this kept up, he didn't stand a prayer of making it through this blow job.

He went to pull out of the wet velvet of Elijah's mouth, but the stretch of a second finger in his ass caused his hips to snap forward, pushing back into the tight cocoon of Elijah's mouth.

Elijah placed a firm hand against Camden's hip, keeping him still, forcing him to experience the dual sensation of being fucked from the inside and out.

The restraint only heightened the experience for Camden. Before, Elijah had given Camden the liberty to tease and torture him in every way Camden could think of. Elijah's only demand was that he be allowed to repay the kindness to Camden when it was his turn to steer them to ecstasy.

Well, Camden relented this go 'round. But karma was a greedy bitch, and he intended to repay every torturous move Elijah doled out. It was only fair. And if Camden believed in anything, it was serving justice.

Elijah curved his tongue, cupping the underside of Camden's cock, caressing each ridge with expert care. As Elijah closed his mouth again, making a tight seal with his lips as they reached the base of Camden's shaft, Camden could feel his balls tighten and inch up. He gave up the idea of payback; the way his muscles were clenching, the way he could hardly think or breathe, Camden was certain he was going to die from the best orgasm he'd ever had, or he was about to have a heart attack. Either way, he didn't think moving on his own accord would be a possibility when Elijah was through with him.

"Not gonna last." Camden's voice sounded ravaged, raw to his ears. But whatever mangled sounds he'd made, Elijah took one long swallow, collapsing his jaws as he sucked his way back up the length of Camden's pole one final time.

He didn't say a word to Camden. He pulled his fingers from Camden's stretched ass and reached for the lube and the single foil packet lying next to it. Once he was sheathed, Elijah poured a generous amount of the lubricant on his cock and used his hand to spread it all over. He took the rest and spread it on his finger, then rubbed the exterior of Camden's hole.

Camden grabbed his sac again. The edge of ecstasy was right there. All Camden had to do was let go, and he'd be at his peak, happily falling into the climax Elijah had led him to. But when he saw Elijah's length straining in the air, Camden tightened his hold on his balls, applying pressure that was just this side of painful to take the edge off. He hadn't been lying when he told Elijah he wanted to come on his cock. After waiting so long to experience that feeling again, the devil himself couldn't have kept Camden away from this particular goal.

Camden groaned as he watched Elijah position the lube bottle over his ass again. He placed his hand on Elijah's arm, preventing him from tipping the bottle over and adding more lubricant. "Trust me, I'm prepped enough, Elijah. I need you inside me now."

Elijah shook his head as he smiled down at Camden. "Nah, baby. I want that ass sloppy wet for me." Elijah moved Camden's hand and poured more lube over his hole, pushing it inside with his wide fingers, making sure Camden's walls were slick and stretched for him. "I need to be balls deep from the first stroke."

ELIJAH consumed the picture of Camden lying spread out on his bed with his balls and dick so flushed with need, his skin had gone from a soft, rosy pink to a deep plum purple. Elijah fought the need to take Camden to the back of his throat again. As much as it would please him to swallow him again, Elijah knew the man couldn't take it. The way he was twitching, fighting to keep from going over the cliff, one well-placed lick was all it would take for him to lose his control and spill his seed all over his belly.

Elijah had made a promise, and he believed in keeping his word, so he bit his bottom lip and stroked his cock, just before sliding carefully inside Camden. Even with all the lubricant and the diligent stretching Elijah had added to their foreplay, the fit was so tight, it stole Elijah's breath. When he'd finally bottomed out, he had to grip the bedrail to keep from falling over onto Camden.

He closed his eyes to savor the viselike grip Camden's body had on his throbbing cock. Five years, and it was still exactly the same as that first night: tempting, self-indulgent, necessary. How could a man he'd only spent a handful of days with feel as important as his next heartbeat? Elijah didn't know the answer to that. He didn't even want to begin to think about why that might be. He wasn't ready to face that, not with so much up in the air between them. The only thing he wanted was to hold on to the moment and make it last for an eternity.

He kept his movements achingly slow at first, taking a second to appreciate every inch Camden's hole swallowed. Elijah pulled back until just his tip remained inside Camden and reveled in the mewling sounds of loss Camden made beneath him. As Camden's hands snaked around, grabbing his ass, pulling him forward, begging for more, Elijah knew his plan to keep this at a slow pace was blown to hell. He held out for as long as he could, but with Camden's hands pushing him forward, his restraint crumbled, and he fell forward into the decadent warmth of Camden's body.

He braced himself on locked arms to keep from crushing Camden as he swerved his hips. The new angle must have been exactly what Camden wanted, because he circled Elijah's back with his arms and pulled him down, flattening rough lips to his as desperate noises fell from his mouth.

If that's what you want, I got you.

Elijah broke the kiss, hooking Camden's legs over his arms and pressing them back, nearly folding him in half. Once Elijah was certain Camden was comfortable in their current position, he moved his hips, each thrust a slightly different angle searching for just the right spot that would put them both over the edge. As Camden's mewling morphed into a rugged growl, Elijah was satisfied he'd found Camden's prostate and continued to pummel the same spot until the walls of Camden's ass began closing around him, strangling his cock.

"Please, please." The single-word litany spilling from Camden's lips kept Elijah on task. No matter how badly his muscles ached from the pace, force, and depth of his thrusts, no matter how desperately he wanted to let go and give in to the climax he could feel tingling at the bottom of his spine, he would keep pumping into Camden until Camden had what he needed. Because as he looked down into the man's pleasure-tortured face, Elijah came to understand that meeting Camden's needs was the only thing that mattered to him. It's what he was made for.

Elijah released Camden's legs, wrapping careful fingers around Camden's cock and sliding his palm down its length. His hand and hips moved in tandem, and Camden broke apart right in front of Elijah's eyes. His body seized and clamped down on Elijah's meat, making his rhythm falter. By the time he'd found his stroke again, Camden's mouth opened, but no sound came out. He closed his eyes just as the first jet of cum left his tip, burying his fingers into Elijah's thighs as each wave of his release crested, fell, and then crested again.

Elijah held on for as long as he could, but all too soon the heaviness in his sac became too much to bear as the buzz of release spread through every nerve in his body. He leaned down, the warm heat of Camden's climax painting his belly as he pressed his lips to Camden's mouth. The kiss was brutal, as was the pounding Elijah's need for completion insisted on.

Elijah knew he would pay for the abuse he was leveling on his injured thigh. He was healed, but there was a fine line between exercise and overuse of a muscle. If he'd been thinking straight, he'd have had Camden riding him to his climax, but having Camden spread open underneath him was too tempting an opportunity to pass up.

Everything about this moment, from the way Camden still grappled through the throes of his own climax to the zing of pleasure that spread through Elijah every time his balls slapped the crack of Camden's ass, reinforced Elijah's inkling that rational thought didn't exist in this scenario.

There was no way it made any sense that having every inch of his cock buried in Camden would feel better than any breath he'd taken in the last five years, including those first ones off of the ventilator after his attack. There was no way Elijah's body should feel more alive than he'd ever been, but simultaneously weaker, more vulnerable than when those hopped-up tweakers tried to stomp the life out of him. How could the simple act of connecting his body with Camden's accomplish such harmony and chaos at the same time?

When Elijah's hips slammed against Camden's ass one last time, as his body seized, and he lost the will to hold back what he knew would be the best nut he'd ever experienced—including the ones Camden had torn from him during their one night together— Elijah realized there was only one reason any of this could be.

Elijah buried his mouth into the curve of Camden's neck and roared as his release took control of him. If they were in his bedroom, Elijah might've been concerned about his mama knowing what naughty things her boy was up to. But here, within the walls of his safe space, his haven, he let go of all the frustration that settled in his chest. He let go of all the pain and misunderstandings that had kept a wedge between him and Camden all of these years. He allowed the joy of this moment to wash over him and pull him into the sheer bliss of having what his heart had always wanted. Camden.

When Camden's arms cradled him into a strong embrace, he dropped his head on Camden's shoulder and nearly sobbed as he tried to draw in his next breath. This place, in the center of Camden's embrace, was always where Elijah was meant to be.

Now, he just needed to convince Camden of that.

Chapter Nineteen

"**TELL** me about your father."

Camden was still half-buzzed from his orgasm, drifting somewhere between sleep and wakefulness as Elijah spooned him from behind. He could've sworn Elijah mentioned something about his father, but with the way Elijah's spent cock rested in the slit of his ass, Camden was too distracted to swear to his own name, let alone the subject of Elijah's question.

"Sorry, didn't catch that." Camden looked over his shoulder to find Elijah's waiting mouth and smiled as he thought of the pleasure it had wrung from him only a handful of moments ago. "What were you asking?"

Elijah tightened the arm he had draped over Camden's bare abdomen and pulled him closer. The solid wall of man pressed against Camden's body was reassuring and comforting like a human body pillow customized specifically for him. Their first night together, there hadn't been any intimate moments of pillow talk. There was just desperate coupling and the exhausted oblivion of postcoital sleep.

"Your dad," Elijah responded. "What's he like?"

Camden took a deep breath before speaking. There were so many ways he could answer that question. There were moments as both a child and an adult that Camden could see how much his father cared for him. He'd always been Camden's greatest cheerleader. Whether it was Camden reciting his lines in a school play or graduating from an Ivy League law school at the top of his class, Michael Warren had pushed his only son to be the best at everything he endeavored. But all of his drive to make Camden perfect at everything often made Camden wonder if his dad pushed him so hard because he doubted Camden's abilities.

"He believes in service. He believes serving in any public capacity is the highest honor any man or woman can hold."

"That sounds admirable." Elijah dropped a quick kiss on Camden's shoulder. "My dad feels the same."

Camden shook his head. These last few days he'd spent in Walter Stephenson's presence showed him the man believed in his boys. He believed in their decisions and their life choices.

Camden was a man well over thirty, and his father didn't seem to think Camden could tie his shoelaces without the older man's guidance.

"Trust me, Elijah, your father might believe in service, but he doesn't appear to demand you serve in the ways he deems appropriate."

"I'm not sure I understand what you mean."

"Let me ask you this. Did you become a cop because your dad demanded it?"

"No." Elijah's answer was quick and succinct. If asked, Camden knew he couldn't respond in the same manner. "I became one because I wanted to work from the inside to build better relations between my community and the police. I hated seeing how communities like mine were being labeled as wastelands because of criminal activity. I hated that the media and often law enforcement seemed to forget that there were good, hardworking people in Brooklyn who deserved their protection and dedication. My father was happy about my choosing to go into the academy, but it was never a requirement."

"You're lucky to have been given the choice." Elijah must've heard the tiny hitch of regret in Camden's voice, because he rose up on his elbow and pulled at Camden's shoulder until Camden turned around and faced him.

"What do you mean by being given the choice, Camden?"

Camden took a deep breath before answering. He'd done his best to not think too much about the path he'd taken into his current career. Dissecting the intricate methods his father used to get Camden to this exact position took more energy than Camden had to spare.

"My father never asked me what I wanted to be. He simply told me where I'd be going to school and what I'd be studying. I think his words were something like, 'Unless you have a way to pay for it, you'll study what I tell you to.'"

"So, you wouldn't have become a lawyer, a prosecutor, without him pushing you?"

Camden didn't know the answer to Elijah's question. He was a damn good prosecutor; knowing the answers to questions and how best to respond to those questions was a large part of his job. One would think a simple inquiry like this wouldn't take much effort on Camden's part. Yet, while Elijah waited for him to reply, Camden ached for someone else to hand him the answer, like a contestant on one of those game shows where he needed to phone a friend.

"There's no easy way to answer that. I'm good at what I do. I enjoy it. Now, I don't know if that's because he forced me onto this path, or if it was because I'm a natural. I just know this life, this plan, is all I've ever had."

Camden could see a spark in Elijah's eyes. Confusion or curiosity, at this point Camden couldn't tell which, mixed in with just a touch of sadness. He waited for Elijah to speak, to fill the gap of silence that appeared to be widening by the minute. But he said nothing, just continued to stare at Camden with his penetrating gaze.

He could feel the warmth of their intimacy being stolen from the room. He grieved its recession and snuggled closer to Elijah to reclaim it. "Please, don't ruin this moment by making me talk about this. The only thing I want is to stay present in the now."

Elijah's gaze softened as he rubbed a gentle thumb over Camden's lips. It was a simple gesture meant to do nothing more than comfort Camden. But the reassuring touch made him feel whole, as if his broken parts were being carefully sewn back together.

"You will always have a choice with me." Elijah pressed his lips against Camden's, then enfolded him into eager arms. Lying there, with his head on Elijah's chest, listening to the lull of his strong heartbeat,

Camden understood, for the first time in his life, what it was to just be yourself with no expectation attached to it. Camden wrapped his arms around Elijah's frame and snuggled deeper into the embrace. He had to savor it now. Once this was all over, there was no telling when Camden would get the chance to experience this again.

"A-YO, Cam, you coming?"

Camden blinked at the sound of Emmanuel's booming voice calling his name. He'd been staring in the bathroom mirror after their shower for what seemed like an eternity. Uncertain what he was looking for, he just knew something was different.

He'd spent two days in Elijah's family's presence, and in that time he'd broken his father's cardinal rule. *No one needs to know the truth but you.*

He'd been trained by the best in evasive maneuvers during questioning. Yet standing with Elijah at his kitchen sink and later on in the garage apartment, he'd spilled everything inside his head and his heart, simply because the man touching him asked for the truth.

Camden and Elijah showered together and dressed before leaving their oasis. Elijah had gone ahead inside the living room while Camden excused himself to the bathroom upstairs just to process the new developments in his connection with Elijah. He couldn't hide forever, since Elijah's mother had caught him halfway up the stairs upon his hasty exit and told him the family was about to watch a movie.

He'd already been on edge from his emotional exchange with Elijah. But hearing Evelyn use the word "family" and knowing she was including him in that number made Camden's already raw nerves cringe with overstimulation.

Fifteen minutes later, Camden was still trying to figure out how he could bow out gracefully. A feigned headache, perhaps? Maybe just plain old-fashion exhaustion would suffice? He shook his head, knowing Elijah would see through any excuse he made.

Camden inhaled slowly through his nose and let the calming breath escape through his pursed lips. He squared his shoulders, gave himself a nod, and resigned himself to feeling awkward and uncomfortable for the next few hours. He had no other choice. Elijah would know he was full of shit if Camden begged off family time. But worse, he'd be let down by Camden's refusal. As long as he lived, Camden knew he never wanted to cause disappointment to cloud Elijah's eyes again.

Camden made his way downstairs and stopped just short of walking inside the family room. The lights were low as the previews had already begun, and Elijah's family had already taken their seats. Elijah's parents were sitting together in the loveseat facing the large, flat-screen mounted above the fireplace. Emmanuel and Vivienne cuddled together on one sofa pushed against the wall, and Elijah stretched out on the remaining sofa on the opposite wall. The only other places available were the two armchairs positioned on either side of the fireplace. But they were facing away from the screen, and he wouldn't be able to watch the movie from that position.

Maybe this was his out? Perhaps the lack of available seating could serve as his excuse to hide in Elijah's bedroom. But just as Cam decided to escape, Evelyn caught sight of him in the doorway.

"Oh, there you are, Camden. The movie's just about to start. Get on in here."

He tried to paste a pleasant smile on his face but wasn't sure he'd accomplished that when he caught Evelyn narrowing her eyes. Too afraid to draw more attention to himself, Camden decided the obvious solution to the problem was to sit on the floor in front of the sofa where Elijah stretched out.

Camden had just nestled himself into a semicomfortable position when Elijah's breath warmed his neck. "You sure you're comfortable down there? This movie is over two hours long, Camden."

A cool shiver spilled down Camden's back as he thought about Elijah's question. The carpet provided some cushion, but not enough that his recently reamed ass wouldn't notice how hard the floor was during a two-hour stretch of sitting on the floor. But what was the alternative? Unless....

"The couch is big enough for the two of us."

Camden looked across the room to where Elijah's brother and sister-in-law were stretched out against the length of the couch, positioned front to back with their legs entangled, and panic struck him. Is that what Elijah expected them to do? Yes, the couch was huge. It had to be custom-made to leave space for anyone else once Elijah lay on it. But as he gave it a quick glance, he could see where the two of them could fit if they positioned themselves in similar fashion to Emmanuel and Vivienne.

Camden swallowed; the thought of being pressed against Elijah's flesh that way made him reconsider Elijah's offer. Getting aroused in front of Elijah's family wasn't his idea of a good time at all.

"Cam, come on."

He imagined every eye in the room was on him even though a quick scan told Camden everyone except he and Elijah was staring at the screen. *Don't make this weird, Camden. You just spent the last hour making love to this man. Why should sharing space with him induce panic?*

Camden knew the answer to that as sure as he knew his own name. Those moments inside Elijah's hideaway were magical, something shared between the two of them. This, sitting here with Elijah's family consuming mindless entertainment, this was real. They had manufactured all the moments they'd shared in front of the Stephensons to keep up the lie they were a couple. But now, even though Camden did not know whether he and Elijah would ever have the chance to become an official couple, the intimacy was no longer a lie.

You can do this. Camden nodded his head, conceding to Elijah's request and stood up. Elijah repositioned himself on the couch so he lay on his side, making room for Camden to slip in front of him. It was strange. The simple move caused both panic and enticement in Camden. Everything in him wanted to be right there cuddled up with Elijah, but the uncertainty of his future, of their future together, gave Camden pause.

For these last few days, he'd played a role for the Stephensons. The only problem that remained was Camden soon realized he didn't want it to be just a role any longer. He was enjoying the closeness he and Elijah were embarking upon. He was enjoying the space the Stephensons made for the man they believed to be Elijah's significant other. But they'd leave by tomorrow evening, and he and Elijah would presumably return to their actual roles of disgruntled cop and annoying

ADA. Or worse, Elijah would press Camden for a commitment he wasn't certain he could make.

"Camden?"

Concern tinted Elijah's voice as he looked up at Camden. The way he said Camden's name, the softness that surrounded the one word, made it seem hallowed, necessary—words Camden had never associated with his own existence before. Hearing it made his heart ache just a little. Here he was with the man of his dreams, being accepted by that man's family, and because of Camden's crazy work life and problematic familial obligations, he might not get to make these moments last beyond this case. *Life really sucks sometimes.*

Camden took the space Elijah had made for him, holding his breath as he pressed himself against the front of Elijah's strong body. It wasn't until Elijah draped his arm over Camden's waist and tugged them closer together that Camden released the breath he'd been holding. He'd been afraid to openly share this kind of intimacy with Elijah, afraid the ruse would be too painful to bear. But the comfort that enveloped him as Elijah's heat cocooned them melted any fear that tried to steal the pleasure of the moment.

Camden took a deep breath as he settled in front of Elijah, letting his warmth chase the chill of fear away. They were in a room full of Elijah's family, and somehow, this moment, this seemingly benign act of sharing a seat in front of the TV was so intimate. Camden had taken part in a lot of sex in his time. But intimacy wasn't something he often engaged in, well, except for the times he and Elijah shared together. Both were more than sex, they were intimate, touching Camden in a way he wasn't prepared for then or now. But as every part of him relaxed into Elijah's embrace, Camden couldn't help but realize the shared intimacy of this moment, even as it played out in front of Elijah's family, didn't bother him at all. No, the intimacy was perfect. The fear of losing it was what held him on edge.

ELIJAH kept his eyes closed as his family filed out of the room. He assumed the movie must be over. The truth was, he hadn't paid attention to the screen since Camden settled in his arms. How could he? Camden was pressed so closely against him that all of Elijah's focus zeroed in on the heady sensation of having Camden in his arms.

Camden had fallen asleep during the movie. Elijah had recognized the rhythmic, even breaths causing his chest to expand and contract halfway through the film. Elijah used the opportunity to gather Camden in his arms, squeezing him tighter than necessary. No one would know, and Camden's heat was so inviting as he pressed himself against Elijah's body, he couldn't resist tightening his hold on the man lying in front of him.

Elijah pretended to sleep too. Having Camden when Elijah was asleep was the only way he could indulge in his need for the man. He was Camden's protector. Being his lover shouldn't feel equally important. And yet somehow they both were necessary to Elijah—as if he had to do both.

He shook the thought from his head and refused to think himself out of the comfort of this moment. They'd shared an amazing moment in the garage. Elijah wasn't about to sour it by thinking about all the problematic things his job and this case could mean for the attachment blossoming between him and Camden.

No, he wouldn't think about the fact that his selfish need to keep Camden close was putting everyone in this house at risk. He refused to acknowledge his job would likely go up in flames when the case was over, all because he couldn't untangle himself from Camden's web. And above all, he most certainly would not admit that when this ended, he'd probably lose more than just his job, but his heart too.

That was too much to ask of any mere mortal. So, for now, he'd enjoy the way Camden's body molded to his.

Elijah knew he should wake Camden, and not just because he had no business being cozied up next to him on the couch. His custom couch fit the two of them comfortably, but Elijah's frame would protest staying in this tight position all night. Rational thought was just about to win out, and Elijah considered waking Camden. But when he pressed himself against Elijah, snuggling in closer to him, he knew they were staying here for the night. Sore back be damned, and regardless of how his rational brain warned him of getting too attached to a man who wasn't in any position to commit to him, Elijah wouldn't give this moment up for anything. This was too good to step away from.

Lying here tonight was a rebirth, even more than the gratifying way they'd shared each other's bodies earlier in the evening. Here and now, they were getting a do-over. And therein lay the danger. What if this feeling was wrong? What if this was the beginning of nothing more than the end?

Chapter Twenty

THE painful pinch of Camden's bladder pulled him from soothing sleep. He opened his eyes just enough to notice he was in the living room, and not in Elijah's bedroom as he should be. He went to maneuver himself into a sitting position but met a comforting weight across his abdomen. A quick peek over his shoulder confirmed what his senses already told him. He'd spent the night in the safest place in the world: Elijah's arms.

The sensual picture of Elijah stretched out behind him with some of his shoulder-length locs covering his face made Camden yearn to reach out and slide his fingers through them. He smiled as he fought the urge to brush the hair behind Elijah's ear. Deciding to let the man sleep longer, he slipped Elijah's hand from around his waist and propped a pillow under it to take his place.

He made haste to Elijah's en suite bathroom and relieved himself. A few minutes later he emerged with an empty bladder, a washed face, and fresh breath. As he opened the bedroom door, he found Elijah's mother standing on the opposite side with her hand poised in the knocking position.

"There you are, Camden. Is Elijah coming down with you?"

Camden shook his head. "He's still sleeping on the couch. I didn't have the heart to wake him when I came up a few moments ago." The wide smile that spread across Evelyn's face made Camden's lips curve in similar fashion. What was it about Elijah and his people that made Camden comfortable enough to share genuine affection with them? He didn't know. But whatever it was, Camden was certain he'd miss it when he went back to his regularly scheduled life.

Evelyn motioned for him to follow her, and because Camden was no fool, he willingly went. They took quiet steps down the staircase. As they eased past the living room, Camden couldn't help but peek inside to check on Elijah. He smiled at the adorable picture the big man made curled up on the sofa, still hugging the small throw pillow Camden had left in his stead.

Satisfied with the tranquil view, Camden followed Evelyn into the kitchen and sat at the island as the woman walked to the refrigerator.

"Do you know how to cook, Camden?"

Camden raised a skeptical eyebrow as he considered how to best answer Evelyn's question. "I can make food that's edible. I wouldn't necessarily classify that as cooking, however."

Camden thought back to when Elijah questioned him about having a maid. Camden conveniently failed to mention his housekeeper cooked for him twice a week. He'd never required Sarah to do it. His work often kept him busy into the late evenings; sometimes he had just enough energy to make it home and sleep. But after having to clean up the remnants of one of his postculinary disasters, Sarah had taken pity on him and offered to prepare him a meal twice a week.

"After grilled cheese or a sliced meat sandwich, I'm a little out of my depth in the kitchen."

Evelyn placed a few covered bowls on the countertop in front of him and spread her hands flat against the hard surface. "Well, if you will spend any significant time around my son, you will need to learn a few things."

Camden laughed softly as he shook his head. The image of Elijah trying to struggle through something Camden prepared was amusing enough to make Camden stifle the chuckle that tried to escape through his lips. "I don't think Elijah needs me trying to cook for him. He seems to know his way around a kitchen, I assume because of you."

Evelyn shook her head and granted him the same warm smile she'd given him when they'd first met. It was hard to believe it was only a few days prior, because the dynamic woman standing in front of Camden felt very much like something permanent in Camden's life.

"Elijah learned to cook while he watched his father and me cooking together. My husband worked late hours most days. But during his time off, he'd do whatever he could to make sure we had some quality time together. He'd play with our boys, and then he'd stand next to me in the kitchen, helping me prepare the family meal."

Her rounded cheeks rose as memory sparkled in her eyes. Whatever events were unfolding in her mind, he realized they were cherished, something she pulled out frequently to enjoy over the years.

The joy Camden received watching Evelyn soon began to dissipate as he thought about the lack of memories he and Elijah shared. As of now, they only had two. The night they'd shared back then, and their time in Elijah's garage apartment last night. Would they be enough for Camden to draw happiness from years down the line when he was trapped in a life not of his own making? Camden's gut clenched in disappointment. He knew the answer to that question was no.

Warm fingers stroked the top of Camden's hand. When he returned his gaze to meet Evelyn's, sweet reassurance greeted him. "Don't worry about how well you do it, Camden. The only thing that will matter is your willingness to do it with him."

Camden narrowed his eyes as he tried to figure out what Evelyn was talking about. He understood her words, but he was certain she was educating him on something vital; he just couldn't figure out what it all had to do with food.

"So, Elijah will want me to cook for him even if my food isn't appetizing?"

Evelyn's face bloomed into a full smile, and he knew for certain whatever message she was trying to impart had gone right over his head. She didn't seem bothered by his ignorance, though; instead, the small chuckle of laughter that escaped her lips showed him she possessed far more patience than he would have if their roles had been reversed.

"I'm not telling you to cook for Elijah. I'm telling you to cook with him. Elijah's interest in cooking as a child was directly related to watching his father and me laugh and play as we prepared family meals. He understood that preparing food was just another way we took care of each other. We loved each other, so we took care of each other. He wanted to be part of the love we shared with each other.

"As independent as Elijah is, he always thrives within a team. Whether it's family, sports, the job, or his friends, Elijah is happiest when he's part of something that's bigger than him. Or haven't you noticed that yet?"

Camden dropped his eyes in shame. He should know that, and if their act had been authentic, Camden would probably have been able to figure that out for himself. He'd seen it with his own eyes how much lighter Elijah's mood was after his family had arrived. Those first twelve hours between the two of them had been awkward to say the least. Elijah had growled more than he spoke to Camden, not that Camden's behavior hadn't warranted that kind of treatment. But Evelyn was right, things had eased between them once Elijah was surrounded by what was most familiar to him, his family.

"So, if you will be the man in Elijah's life, cooking with him is something you must do."

Slight panic set in in the middle of Camden's chest. Yes, things between him and Elijah had taken a decided turn for the better. Yes, they both wanted more than just that one moment in time. But neither of them had concluded precisely what more meant. Elijah's desire to be with Camden was easy as long as they were in this little cocoon in Westchester. But once they both returned to life in Brooklyn, would Elijah want to take on the battle of wills with Camden's father? It was too great a deal to ask of one individual. Not to mention, Camden wasn't certain he deserved that kind of loyalty from Elijah, not after everything he'd put him through.

"As much as Elijah and I care for each other, we haven't yet decided on anything regarding our relationship. It's complicated."

Evelyn tipped her head to the side, watching Camden, using what he assumed was her sixth mother's sense that Elijah had described earlier. Alarm spread through him. He was a trained prosecutor, someone who knew how to read people and keep them from reading him. However, sitting there under this petite woman's gaze, it was as if she knew all his truths, no matter how he tried to hide them.

"You young people, always making things more difficult than they need to be." Evelyn waved a dismissive hand through the air before she leaned down and pulled a cast-iron skillet from the cabinet. She rinsed it, set it on the stovetop, and turned on the range. When she was done, she pulled a platter from another cabinet and set it between them on the island. "The only thing that matters is how you and Elijah feel about each other. All of this complicated stuff isn't important."

Camden lifted a disbelieving brow as he watched her arrange all the items on the counter in the order she preferred. "If you knew what our issues were, I think you might say different, Mrs. Stephenson."

Evelyn held her pointer finger into the air and said, "Evelyn, or Mama if you'd prefer."

Camden's mouth hung open in response. Not that he'd have a problem using the term to address Evelyn Stephenson. Her warmth, her concern, made it easy to see mothering was her specialty. He'd known her for just a few days, and she'd soothed him in ways his own mother had never managed to. Yet he still hesitated to take that liberty. No, he couldn't address her that way when he wasn't certain if being with Elijah was even a possibility at this point.

Fortunately for Camden, Evelyn had pulled her gaze from Camden's face and set about uncovering the bowls she'd placed on the counter, so she didn't see the way his mouth was hanging open at the moment.

He shook his head, giving himself a second to compose himself before he spoke again. "Evelyn, Elijah and I have a great deal to work on. No matter how wonderful these last few days have been, they haven't fixed all the problems Elijah and I have to figure out."

The matron gave Camden an easy smile as she leaned forward, placing both her elbows on the counter, bracing her chin on her opened palms. "Did you cheat on my son? Were you abusive to him, emotionally, sexually? Did you put your hands on my baby?"

Camden shook his head as the questions spilled from the sweet curve of her lips. Her tone was so light and sugary, what you'd expect coming from a loving matriarch. But he could tell by the squint of her eyes she was tuned in, waiting for Camden's answers.

"No, Evelyn. Our struggles had nothing to do with any of the things you just mentioned. And in case you're wondering, those things would never be a concern for Elijah and me."

She kept the same inviting smile on her face and nodded her head. "I didn't think so. But a mother always has to worry, even when her child is the burly protector type."

Camden chuckled at her apt description of Elijah. He was big, beautiful, and fierce, in all the best ways, and if there was one thing Camden understood from his interactions with Evelyn Stephenson, it was that her son hadn't inherited just her smile, but her heart and spirit too.

"My point about those questions is this, Camden. Those things are deal breakers. Those are the kinds of problems that keep people apart even when they love each other. If your problems aren't those, then they're not that complicated at all. As I see it, it just comes down to one thing. How badly do you want it?"

The question was simple, and yet Camden couldn't fashion an answer for it. He knew Evelyn had no way of comprehending what sort of obstacles rested in the gap between Camden and Elijah. But somehow the confidence with which she spoke was comforting, like a down throw on a chilly night in front of a fire, the kind of comfort one experienced when they were covered in absolute truth.

"Camden, my son is there. If you know what signs to look for, it's easy to tell he's ready to give you everything. The only problem is, you don't seem sure of whether you want what he's offering. If you wanted him to, Elijah would chase you to the ends of the earth. You just have to decide if you want to be caught."

She winked an eye at Camden, then pointed at the bowls on the counter. "Go get yourself an apron out of the pantry. I'm gonna show you how to make salmon croquettes and biscuits for my boy."

"I thought you said it didn't matter if I could cook or not, that Elijah wanted me to cook with him, be part of his team?"

Evelyn's body shook with laughter. Even after she composed herself, happiness shone in the depths of her dark brown eyes. "Yes, honey. All of that was true. But what's also true is that the quickest way to any man's heart is a good meal he didn't have to prepare himself. Get on in here so I can show you how to get and keep your man."

Not the least bit embarrassed by his eagerness to get to Evelyn's side, Camden walked around the counter and wrapped his arms around Evelyn in much the same way she'd done to him upon their initial meeting. Hugging it out wasn't exactly Camden's modus operandi, but nothing else made sense at the moment. So he stood there, well past the time when it would've been polite to release her, and hugged Elijah's mother like he'd never had the chance to hug his own.

Chapter Twenty-One

FAMILIAR scents from his childhood invaded Elijah's dreams, settling into the happy space where memories of Saturday morning breakfasts with his family were stored. Those moments where his father's presence filled the house, and how they interacted as a complete unit, defined what family meant to him.

Those Saturdays began as early as his school days, but Elijah didn't whine about getting up for them. Once he heard music filling the house, Elijah would jump out of bed, wash his face and brush his teeth, and run down the stairs.

He could always tell who was cooking by what kind of music he heard playing. His father's Caribbean roots dictated that fast-paced calypso or the heavy bass of dance-hall reggae would saturate the air. But if he heard old-school R&B or gospel, his mother was at the helm and more than likely making Elijah's favorite meal.

Elijah tried to settle back into sleep, but the distinctive intro the Isley Brothers' "For the Love of You" began, and Elijah's eyes popped open. He blinked to clear his vision and stopped to listen for Ronald Isley's smooth tenor begin that all too popular, classic first line of the song. A few seconds later, Ronald didn't disappoint.

He swung his legs off the couch and stood too quickly. Elijah didn't let the discomfort stop him. If his mama was in his kitchen cooking biscuits and salmon cakes, he wouldn't be the only one in the house to realize it. If he wanted to snatch as many croquettes as his belly could handle, he'd have to beat his big-headed brother to the table first.

A mad dash up the stairs and a few minutes at his bathroom vanity, and Elijah was presentable enough to sit at his table. He stopped in the kitchen doorway to take in a deep breath. "I swear, Mama, every time you come up here I gain ten pounds. You can't keep feeding me like—"

Elijah stopped talking when he saw Camden standing in front of the stove, tending to a sizzling cast-iron skillet. He seemed odd, out of place. He could probably tell you the difference between a salad fork and a dinner fork, and where they should be positioned in a place setting. But few people knew how to cook with a cast-iron skillet. That shit took skill built on years of practice. The care instructions alone demanded a mastery most kitchen novices wouldn't know how to accomplish.

His shoulders were stiff, and he held the spatula at a weird angle that didn't seem like the most efficient way to scoop or flip a salmon cake in hot grease. It was amusing to see this man who always looked so put together—even when he was puttering around the house in Elijah's borrowed clothes—with an old apron tied around his waist and his hair hanging into his face as he watched the sizzling patties carefully.

Awkward and unsure as he may be, he was doing it right. Well, the kitchen wasn't filled with smoke, and nothing was on fire, so he assumed Camden was doing it right. Warmth spread through Elijah at the disheveled sight of Camden. It was hard to imagine, but his uncertainty in Elijah's kitchen made him even sexier than before.

As adorable as Camden was at his stove, Elijah knew there was only one reason they weren't choking on smoke right now. He took in the scene, scanning the room, looking for the only plausible explanation for this "fish out of water" scene. His search landed on his mother sitting at the kitchen table, sipping on a cup of coffee and munching from a plate stacked with salmon cakes and biscuits.

Elijah walked over to the table and greeted his mother with a kiss to her cheek. "What's that about?" She looked up at him, following the finger he had pointed to Camden at the stove.

"Last I checked, they called it making breakfast, son." Elijah glanced over at Camden, who lifted his head long enough to greet Elijah with a smile and then returned his focus to the skillet in front of him.

"You mean you let Camden make my salmon cakes?" Elijah paused at the disappointment in his own voice. His voice took on that whiny sound that only an annoyed kid could produce when talking to his parents. "Ma, you know I love those."

"You do know I can hear you, right, Elijah?" Camden's question didn't sway him. As cool as Camden was, Elijah doubted the man could replicate his mother's skill when it came to this dish. There were just some foods only certain people got to make, and salmon cakes were always made by his mother.

"Camden, I'm sure you've tried really hard, but I'm not about to let you mess this up for me. My mouth is all the way fixed for some salmon cakes this morning. I ain't even about to play with you."

Camden moved the frying salmon cakes from the skillet onto a platter. He turned the range off, then brought the batch of food over to the table. "Why don't you at least taste one before you insult my cooking?"

Elijah looked at his mother, then returned his gaze to Camden. He narrowed his eyes before snatching one of the golden-brown croquettes out of the plate. "Salt and pepper is not seasoning. If that's all I taste, I swear I will get my gun." Elijah took an angry bite and chewed. "Got me in here eating bland-ass salmon cakes early in the morning."

He was about to say something else when his taste buds recognized the familiar savory flavors filling his senses. He thought it had to be a fluke. No way could Camden, or anyone else as far as Elijah was concerned, cook this signature dish like his mama. He popped the last bit into his mouth, waiting to be proved right. But as he chewed, he could feel the satisfied groan climbing from his chest, looking for an escape through his lips. Elijah went to grab a second cake from the serving platter, but Camden placed a hand on his arm and stared at him with a skeptical lifted brow. "What?" Elijah chimed with a mouthful of food. "I'm just making sure they're not poisonous. It's my job to serve and protect."

Camden folded his arms in front of his chest as he leveled his gaze at Elijah. Apparently, he wasn't buying

Elijah's bullshit about checking for poison in the food. "A'ight, I can't lie, these are good."

Elijah swallowed, humming not so quietly as he savored each bite. He knew Camden had a smartass "I told you so" waiting for him. He didn't care in the least. This was his favorite dish, and a man who was becoming more likable by the hour had toiled to gift him with this spread. Showing his appreciation by humming was the bare minimum Elijah could do at the moment.

The oven timer dinged, pulling Camden away from the table and giving Elijah the chance to slide into the seat next to his mother. "How'd you get him to slave in the kitchen?"

His mother shook her head, then sipped from her cup of coffee. "It's salmon cakes and biscuits, Elijah, not a seven-course meal. I don't think slaving is an accurate description."

He took the serving tongs and placed several of the fried patties on his plate. He'd pay for these later in the gym, but for now, he'd eat until his stomach couldn't hold any more. "I've made these before, Mama. They ain't as easy as you make them out to be, especially without a deep fryer. You've got that boy in there sweating over hot grease and the inferno of the oven. How'd you do it?"

Elijah was partially distracted as he watched Camden bend over to remove what looked like another batch of his mother's homemade biscuits. Elijah licked his lips, not sure if it was because of the food or the perfect way his sweatpants molded Camden's ass. He didn't have the chance to figure out which before he heard his mother chuckling beside him.

"I know this might be a strange concept to you, son. But you'd be surprised what you can get people to do if you simply ask."

Elijah glanced at his mother and watched as she used her coffee mug to hide the glib smile on her face. Asking. It seemed like a simple thing. Except there was nothing simple about him and Camden. Yeah, they'd talked, and talking made it so much easier for Elijah to give in to the very thing he desired. But knowing what you wanted and knowing you could have it were two different things.

There was no doubt in Elijah's mind he wanted Camden. If Camden gave him the chance, Elijah would do all he could to explore what they shared. All he needed was the opportunity, and Elijah could move mountains if he put his mind to it.

His mother's soft hand rested on top of his as she stood up from the table. "I already took some plates downstairs to Manny and Viv, and one upstairs to your father. I think it's gonna be a lazy day for everyone in the house until we leave tonight. Maybe now might be a perfect time for you to kiss the cook?"

Elijah squinted his eyes and looked up to her. "Now see, that seemed like a fantastic idea before my mama said it. No man wants to hear things like that coming from their mom."

Evelyn waved a dismissive hand at him before she spoke again. "Boy, how do you think you got here?"

Elijah covered his ears with his hands as he shook his head back and forth. "Nope, nope, nope. We will not have this discussion. You will not ruin sex for me for the rest of my life by putting that image in my head."

Camden returned to the table, looking from Elijah to Evelyn and back as he tried to decipher what was going on. "What exactly did I miss?"

"Just my grown child behaving like a two-year-old. I'll leave him in your capable hands, Camden. I'm gonna make a quick run to the market so I can teach

Camden how to make your favorite dinner before we
leave tonight."

"Give me a minute to throw some clothes on, and
I'll take you, Ma."

Evelyn shook her head. "It's just at the corner,
Elijah. I can handle carrying a few bags up the street.
You stay here and enjoy the quiet."

As the closing front door clicked behind her,
Elijah stared at the man standing next to him. Camden
gleamed with laughter, his shoulders were loose, and
the hard planes of his face were smoothed by the
brightness of his smile. The smile was so inviting,
Elijah grabbed Camden by the hand and pulled him
down until Camden was sitting in his lap.

"Thank you for all of this. It was a thoughtful
gesture." It was a simple act, but from Camden, someone
Elijah was becoming more emotionally entangled with
by the hour, its meaning ran much deeper than that. It
was comfort, a reminder that he was safe and taken care
of. Which was strange, considering Camden was the
one who needed reassurance in this scenario.

The kitchen was a place he was either alone or where
he was cooking to care for others. Besides his family, no
one had ever taken care of him. In this one deed, Camden
fed more than Elijah's stomach. He'd filled his soul.

"I really enjoyed it. I hope you didn't let my mother
pressure you into cooking this morning."

Camden slid his arm around Elijah's neck, fingering
his locs. "Your mom could pretty much convince me of
anything. I think she could out-lawyer even me. But I
was happy to learn how to cook your favorite meal. It's
the least I could do."

Camden continued to stroke Elijah's hair as their
gazes connected. It was strange, the soothing way the
simple repetitive motion made Elijah tighten his hold on

Camden. Elijah didn't allow many people to touch his hair. He wasn't one of those dudes who allowed people to pet him like he was some oddity to be examined. But the simple way Camden touched his hair, as if it were something to be revered, made Elijah's chest fill with the warmth and comfort that only came with the first buds of blossoming trust.

As smiling blue eyes look down at him, he recognized who he held in his arms. This wasn't the man who walked out on him. This was a new man. The man Elijah was falling in love with.

Acknowledging that should've scared the hell out of Elijah. They were hiding out in his house because someone was trying to kill Camden, and according to Camden, even if they survived the Path, Camden's father would never allow them to be together. Either of those things should've made Elijah run. But being here with Camden like this forced Elijah to admit the truth. There wasn't anything that would make him run from Camden. Why would he when Camden possessed everything Elijah needed to survive? Camden held his heart.

He pressed a quick kiss to Camden's cheek and nuzzled the curve of Camden's neck as he thought of the words his mother had gifted him with. Maybe Evelyn Stephenson was right. Perhaps he would be surprised at the answer if he got up the nerve to ask Camden for the commitment he wanted. Maybe if Elijah pushed everything aside, he could find the strength to tell Camden exactly what he needed.

"If I had known fried ground fish patties would make you this happy, I'd have asked your mom for the recipe the first night your family arrived."

Elijah pulled back just enough to take in the sight of Camden. Serenity beamed outward from the sparkle in his eye to the brightness of his smile. Camden was happy.

Whether he noticed it in himself, Elijah didn't know. But watching Camden as he reclined in his embrace told Elijah all he needed to recognize it. Whatever dreams Elijah had for tomorrow, Camden shared them.

"Why wouldn't I be happy? I've got everything I want. My mother's salmon cakes and biscuits, and you."

A faint rose tint colored Camden's cheeks as he closed his eyes. His long lashes fanning against the apples of his reddened cheeks made Elijah's heart swell at the thought his words could have a physical impact on Camden.

"Your sister-in-law was right. You really are a sweet talker."

There was no sense in denying the truth. Elijah's charm, when it came to flirting, was a proven fact. He wasn't much of a talker in most situations, but when it came to pulling the interest of a man, Elijah's tongue was magic.

"Can't lie, your man got game for days. But that wasn't a line, Camden."

Camden stiffened in Elijah's arms, the easy smile he wore disappearing as he focused his attention on Elijah. "Then what was it?"

Elijah took a deep breath before speaking, trying to steady his heartbeat. For a moment, Elijah thought his heart was racing because of resurfacing fears. But sitting here in the quiet corner of his kitchen with Camden gathered in his arms, Elijah realized what he was feeling was excitement, anticipation, and hope.

"A request—" Elijah opened his mouth to let the question burning in his heart make its way to the air, but then he stopped to take in the vision of Camden. A slightly crooked smile softened the sharp angles of Camden's face, warming Elijah's heart.

He took a slow, cautious breath, afraid to disturb the moment in even the slightest of ways. He'd spent five years trying to erase the night he'd shared with

Camden from his memory, and now, he'd give anything to preserve this moment where Camden sat in his lap, melting him from the inside out.

"Elijah, everything all right?"

For the first time in a long time, everything in his world was perfect. His home was filled with love and laughter, and the center of all that comforting heat had radiated from the man in Elijah's arms. The timing was wrong, the situation was for shit, but everything about the way Camden made him feel was so incredibly right, Elijah ached at the thought of losing it when this was all over.

"I know this is the worst possible time, Camden." Elijah picked up one of Camden's hands, turning it palm-side up, placing a gentle kiss in it. "But when this is all over, I need us to have a conversation."

Camden's smile faded slightly as his eyebrow rose. "Regarding?"

Elijah kissed his palm again, savoring the tiny shiver rippling through Camden's body in response. "Us. I need us to be very clear about where this is going."

"As far as I remember, Elijah, my calendar is open for the next couple of days. I'm sure I can make time for a heart-to-heart anytime you like."

Elijah shook his head. Although the thought of spilling the contents of his heart this very minute made Elijah's pulse jump with excitement, he knew now wasn't the time. There was too much going on, and Camden was too dependent on Elijah for his survival for either of them to be certain that this growing bond was born of their need for each other instead of the severity of the situation.

"Not the right time," Elijah answered. "Too much going on. But the second this is over, I need us to lay our cards on the table. No running this time."

Camden dropped his chin and closed his eyes. The lure of his cocky grin was gone, replaced by what looked to be shame.

"Elijah, I—"

Elijah released Camden's hand and placed a single finger over his lips, silencing him before he could continue speaking.

"You weren't the only one running, baby. I'm a cop. Finding you, tracking you down for answers would've been a simple task with my background. Instead, I let my bruised ego get the better of me. I knew what we were the minute your lips touched mine. And yet, I was so afraid of rejection, I gave up without fighting. Not this time. This time, I'm not letting you walk away before I've said my piece."

Elijah cupped Camden's cheek in his palm, softly stroking the morning stubble beneath his thumb, loving the mild hint of gruffness it gave his gentleman. "Is that all right with you, Mr. Assistant District Attorney?"

A quick nod and a smile was Camden's only response as he leaned in to kiss Elijah. Elijah covered Camden's mouth with his hand and shook his head. "Salmon cakes are great for eating, but not so much for kissing. Give me a few minutes to freshen up, and then we'll finish this in the garage."

Camden's eyes sparked with amusement as a quiet chuckle slipped through his closed lips. He pressed a kiss to the inside of Elijah's palm and removed the hand from his mouth.

"You have the best ideas, Lieutenant."

"If you think that's something, wait until you hear my next suggestion, then."

Camden licked his lips. The tiny bit of his rosy tongue sliding across the fullness of his bottom lip made Elijah's cock tighten in his shorts. "Whatever it is, Elijah, I can't wait to hear it."

Chapter Twenty-Two

CAMDEN looked around the one-room garage apartment and smiled. It wasn't small, but Camden was certain it could fit inside the room he'd slept in as a child in his parent's mansion, ten times over.

His mother would call it cozy or some other snobby description, he was sure. But to Camden, since the first time Elijah had shared this space with him, he'd felt more cared for, more cherished than he'd ever experienced in his life.

The sound of the bathroom faucet being turned off pulled Camden from his musings. He cupped his hands together, blowing into them and making sure that the toothpaste and mouthwash he'd used a few moments ago were working. The tastiness of breakfast aside, Camden was glad to have his palate cleansed. The only thing he wanted to taste was Elijah, and if he had his way, that's exactly what he'd get to do in "Five, four, three, two...."

"Now, we're all minty fresh."

Camden turned around to greet a smiling Elijah. "Good, so can we make out now?"

Elijah's shoulders shook with laughter. "You know, I hope you don't think every time I bring you here it's only to sex you, Cam."

"I'd be offended if that wasn't the reason you were bringing me here." Camden stepped closer into Elijah's space, running his fingers along the hem of Elijah's T-shirt and dragging it until deep mahogany-brown skin filled his vision and made Camden's heart race with desire.

Elijah was a beautiful man. He was tall, solid, his muscles large and defined. But when Camden's gaze traveled from the sharp angles of V-cut hips, to carved abdominal muscles, to beyond his expansive chest and strong shoulders, he realized something in retrospect that he hadn't allowed himself to see before. It wasn't that Elijah's glorious body weakened Camden and made him feel helpless. Nor was it the soft welcome that Camden always saw in the depths of Elijah's eyes that touched him most.

It had been there that first night. Camden had known no matter what, Elijah accepted him for who he was, a self-centered, often selfish individual who didn't deserve the affections of an honest man like Elijah.

Elijah's dark brown eyes radiated warmth, inviting Camden in from the cold mausoleum he'd existed in all these years. He wrapped his hand around Elijah's waist and pulled him closer until there was no space between them.

Camden placed tiny kisses on the side of Elijah's neck, just under his ear. He could feel a smile spreading across Elijah's face as he continued to pepper the man's neck and jaw with sweet pecks of his lips.

"What am I going to do with you, Cam?"

"Whatever you want to. I'm yours any way you'll have me."

Before Elijah could respond, Camden locked his fingers in Elijah's hair and slammed his mouth against Elijah's in an almost painful press of lips.

Elijah remained stiff in his arms, probably wondering why the crazy man holding him was attacking his mouth. It wasn't until Elijah's lips parted slightly, and Camden took the opportunity to slide his tongue inside Elijah's heat, that the muscles in Elijah's body began to relax as he pressed himself closer to Camden.

Elijah moaned, granting Camden the access he needed to deepen the kiss. If he was too chickenshit to tell Elijah how desperate he was to have a chance with him, to keep him near like a life-giving breath, he'd at least show him. He'd make sure every touch conveyed every word he was too afraid to speak.

Camden walked them back toward the daybed, hoping they'd make it, but happily settling for the carpeted floor when need outweighed common sense. If this ended up being as frantic as Camden surmised it would, they were both going to regret this decision to fuck on the floor like animals. But if the choice was being rational and walking to the bed like sane human beings, or feeling the delicious grind of Elijah's stiff cock moving against his, Camden would deal with the rug burn tomorrow.

He wasted no time divesting Elijah and himself of their clothing, releasing a satisfied moan when flesh met flesh, searing Camden from the outside in.

He took a moment just to revel in the heat they generated as they rubbed against each other. It was hot, primal, full of so much need, Camden thought he might combust from the sparks of electricity sizzling through his body.

"Baby, please," Elijah begged in short gasps, apparently breathing and speaking at the same time were a struggle at the moment. "Won't last like this."

Camden slowed his rhythm, letting one of his hands slide down the length of Elijah's torso, loving the feel of smooth skin beneath his fingertips. He kept his movements slow, allowing his lips to touch the places where his hand had preceded his mouth.

The intricate pattern of the tattoo ink that covered Elijah's left pectoral muscle mesmerized him, its long lines branching out to his shoulder and winding together as it circled his left arm. Camden stopped just above the pec, placing a gentle kiss over the strong thumping of Elijah's heartbeat.

Its cadence was soothing to Camden. Not so long ago Camden had stood next to Elijah's hospital bed, fearful that he'd never feel the vibrant, steady beat again.

He'd snuck into Elijah's room every night under the pretense of official prosecutorial business, praying and willing Elijah's heart to keep beating another day.

Elijah's doctors might disagree, but Camden believed his daily ritual of standing by that bed, demanding that Elijah live for no other reason than Camden needed him to, had as much to do with Elijah's recovery as the medical and surgical interventions provided by the healthcare team.

Tonight, it beat wildly in Elijah's chest, the rhythm once again yielding to Camden's need for Elijah to live, to thrive.

Camden's mouth moved down to Elijah's nipple, a satisfying moan escaping both their lips as soon as Camden's tongue met the stiff peak. He closed his eyes and let himself delight in the needy sounds coming from Elijah beneath him.

Those sounds were raw, guttural, pleading with Camden for more. Elijah didn't have to worry. Camden would give him everything he desired. How could he not when satisfying Elijah was all he craved?

He'd spent so much time telling himself that it was only a night, that it was meaningless. But he'd always known the truth. Somewhere deep down beneath all his bullshit, Camden's soul had longed to reunite with Elijah's.

He was here now, bonded with the man he'd ached for, needed like precious life-giving air. He was here, and he knew regardless of what the outside world held, he was never willingly giving Elijah up again.

Camden continued to pepper kisses down Elijah's chest, licking down the hard, sculpted landscape of Elijah's abdomen, until he reached beyond his navel and met the wet tip of his cock.

Cut, the domed cap straining with need. Camden licked his lips, his tongue eager for a taste. He'd been so needy the last time they were in this room, that he hadn't taken the opportunity to worship Elijah's cock with his mouth. He wouldn't make that mistake again.

Camden swirled his tongue around the cap and eased his mouth slowly down Elijah's considerable length. He moaned at the indecent stretch of his lips as he continued his descent.

He only made it halfway before his scalp prickled where Elijah's strong fingers grasped his hair. When Elijah's raspy "Please" filled the air, Camden wrapped his fingers around the wide base of Elijah's cock, and continued his journey until his lips met his hand.

He worked his hand and his mouth in tandem to maximize Elijah's pleasure, a tactic that was working as indicated by the frantic way Elijah thrust his hips forward every time Camden's mouth sank lower, swallowing him.

Camden let two of his fingers slip inside his mouth. With Elijah's girth, it was a tight fit, but the lube was too far away at the moment. If this would go beyond devouring Elijah's cock, he'd eventually have to get up. But the taste of Elijah's flesh on his tongue had Camden's dick so hard, moving from his current position wasn't something he could entertain.

The next time Elijah thrust upward, Camden let a single, slick finger slip slowly into Elijah's ass. He took his time sliding in and out until Elijah choked out an impatient, "More."

Determined to please him, Camden added another finger, scissoring and stretching Elijah. The resulting mewling sounds spilling into the air made Camden's blood boil with desire.

Camden pulled Elijah from his mouth as he leveled his gaze upon his lover. The sight of him, locs free, creating a midnight halo around Elijah's head, made the breath catch in Camden's chest. His body was sculpted and beautiful, muscles tense with need. His legs were spread wide, welcoming Camden's touch so deep inside him. There was nothing as magnificent as the picture of need this amazing man embodied.

I want to be the only one to make him need this way. Always.

The realization of the thoughts tumbling in his head made his movements come to a standstill. The loss of stimuli made Elijah slowly open his eyes.

"Cam?"

Camden shook his head, trying to break free of his thoughts, desperate to return to the moment. "Sssh," he whispered. "I was just getting supplies." He removed his fingers and leaned over Elijah, placing a quick peck on his lips, before getting up on his knees and leaning over to reach the nightstand they'd landed in front of.

Supplies in hand, he sheathed himself, coating his covered cock in lube, then doing the same to his fingers. He continued to stretch Elijah, making certain he was prepared for Camden. He was desperate to seat himself inside Elijah. But caring for him this way took precedence over his desire.

Camden restrained himself until Elijah grabbed his cock and stroked himself in tandem with Camden's caresses. The sight of Elijah so lost in his pleasure, his muscles gripping Camden's fingers with tight spasms, his bottom lip held hostage by his teeth as Elijah succumbed to the sensual rhythm of it all, made Camden's cock throb with an almost painful ache.

He pulled his fingers free and fought to control his need to bottom out from his first stroke. Instead, he fed Elijah's hole one unhurried inch of himself at a time and nearly collapsed from the necessary control the restraint demanded.

Camden tried to remain still and gather his strength. His resolve didn't last long; as Elijah's muscles squeezed his cock, he pulled back and pushed forward with no help from him.

"God, I've missed this."

"Me too," Elijah muttered, penetrating the heavy haze of Camden's lust-drunk mind. In truth, he'd been so taken by the glorious sensation of Elijah's ass strangling his fucking cock, he hadn't realized he'd spoken those four words aloud until he heard Elijah's response.

He leaned forward, deepening his stroke, changing his angle each time he plunged inside, seeking the tiny electric knot he knew would be Elijah's undoing. He continued searching for the perfect angle when Elijah's moans became louder, building from a quiet whimper to a pronounced outcry of pleasure.

Camden pulled out, motioning for Elijah to turn over. He complied quickly, dropping his shoulders to the floor, his hair spread across the floor in a wild heap, his ass tempting Camden as Elijah swayed his hips back and forth, beckoning Camden to return.

Camden leaned down, stopping to worship Elijah's full, hanging sac, wondering how he could've ever been foolish enough to walk away from this. It wasn't just the sex; it wasn't just the beauty of the man beneath him. It was need. Since his first taste of this man, need crawled into his system, spread through his blood, and embedded itself in his DNA. His body craved Elijah like it did air, and depriving himself of him had damaged his heart, over time slowly killing off the parts that made it beat properly.

He seated himself again, one thrust to the hilt, and he was bottoming out again. The new position allowed him deeper penetration. Elijah whimpered beneath him, his fingers searching for purchase in the short fibers of the carpet as Camden plunged in and out of him. Camden loved facing his partner during sex. But the sight of Elijah coming undone on Camden's cock

while on all fours was breathtaking. Not to mention the pushback Elijah gave as he met each snap of Camden's hips with an equal rock of his own had Camden glad he was already on his knees.

How could one man have so much power over Camden that even the breathless sounds he made while they rutted touched Camden in the deepest parts of him? There was only one answer.

He loved him.

Camden loved the man who welcomed him into the most intimate parts of his body. He loved the man who'd brought him to his home even though this was supposed to be just a job. He loved the man whose family had taken him in as one of their own simply because they thought Camden held Elijah's heart.

In a long weekend, Camden experienced more love in the presence of the Stephensons than he had in a lifetime. And with his cock sliding in and out of Elijah's body, Camden realized he never wanted to leave Elijah, his home, or the Stephensons.

Camden wanted it all. It didn't matter he didn't deserve it, that he hadn't proven his worth to Elijah or the wonderful people back in the house who loved him. Camden wanted all of this to be his. No, he wanted it to be theirs.

Camden leaned down, covering Elijah's back with his body, as if he were a human blanket.

He needed to be closer. His cock was buried inside Elijah, his balls pressed tightly against Elijah's taint, but it still wasn't deep enough for him. It still wasn't enough of a connection. He needed more.

Camden swept Elijah's locs away from his face, placing kisses anywhere his mouth could reach. And when Elijah turned his head enough so that their lips

could meet in an awkward side kiss, messy, sloppy wet with tongues clashing, Camden thought he'd collapse from the satisfaction of being joined with Elijah in every way he knew how.

Elijah broke the kiss first. "Please," he begged. "So close."

Camden kissed Elijah's face again, soothing him with each gentle peck, promising to give him everything he wanted. And Camden would. He'd give everything to Elijah, because from the first night they'd met, from the first time Elijah's wide grin had spread across full lips, Camden had known Elijah should always be happy.

He'd fucked that up the first go 'round. But Camden would be damned if he'd mess this up again. No, now, he would get it right no matter what the cost to himself.

Camden lifted himself off Elijah's back, reaching his arm around his waist, wrapping sure fingers around Elijah's straining cock.

Each stroke of Camden's hand matched the rhythm of each thrust of his hips. He bit his lip, trying to take the edge off his orgasm, determined that the trembling man beneath him would be satisfied first.

Camden switched his angle, feeling Elijah's muscles tighten around him like an unforgiving vise. He held his breath, fighting the orgasm sparking at the base of his spine until Elijah's cock pulsed in his hand. The first jet of cum coated Camden's fingers in a thick, hot rope.

Camden continued to work Elijah until he was spent, his muscles so weak with satisfaction he stretched out completely on the floor, nearly unseating Camden as he slid into the prone position.

Camden braced his arms on the floor and gave in to the need burning through his body like liquid

fire, consuming him from the inside. He snapped his hips, letting Elijah's orgasm spark his own. His balls tightened, drawing up tight against his body just before his muscles seized, and his breath caught in his chest.

When the burn of release clawed through him, Camden shut his eyes, giving in to the blinding need to let go. His cock pulsed, and the heady rush of satisfaction pulled him under with each spurt inside the latex barrier covering his cock.

His muscles held him up just past the last pulse of his orgasm, and he landed gracelessly on top of Elijah. In his mind he told himself he should probably move. But when Elijah's hand gripped the back of his thigh, Camden decided being sprawled across a willing partner was exactly what he needed in this moment.

Why mess with perfection?

Chapter Twenty-Three

CAMDEN turned over in the bed and winced at the tenderness in his ass. He'd thought he'd had the upper hand when he'd had Elijah spread on the floor, pummeling into the depths of his heat. He should've known it was only a temporary victory.

Elijah gifted him with a twenty-minute reprieve before he had Camden pinned to the mattress, screaming into the pillows, fearful and yet hopeful of the fact he was certain he was being split in two.

His body was tired, but he found just enough strength to curve his lips into a lazy smile as he joined gazes with Elijah.

"Hey," Camden greeted him before leaning over to place a quick kiss on Elijah's lips. "You think we could stay out here forever?"

Elijah wrapped a lazy arm around Camden's waist and pulled him closer. "I'd love to, but if we miss my mama's smothered pork chops, potato salad, and sweet potato pie, neither of us will have to worry about the Path, because Evelyn Stephenson will kill us."

Camden rested his head on Elijah's chest, chuckling softly at the idea of the barely five-foot woman doing them bodily harm. "How on earth do you stay as fit as you are and eat like that?"

"Did you not see the gym in my basement? With a cooking mama like mine, that's a necessity, not a luxury."

"You're so lucky your mom takes care of you the way she does. That woman is a saint. I don't care what you say, I couldn't imagine her harming anyone."

Camden's head bounced a little when Elijah's chest rumbled with laughter. "My hind parts would beg to differ." Elijah snuggled closer to Camden. "The tenderness I feel from having you ride me into bliss is nothing compared to the switch she used to take to my ass when I was acting a damn fool."

"I don't believe that sweet woman ever hurt you. She loves you too much."

"She does, but that didn't stop her from reining me in when she needed to."

Warmth spread through him as he watched an inviting smile tilt the corners of Elijah's mouth upward. Whatever the differences in their childhoods, it was clear Elijah and his mother shared a loving connection that Camden both praised and envied at the same time.

Elijah slid a teasing hand down the curve of Camden's ass, squeezing gently when he reached the meaty swell. "We've been ghost most of the day.

We should at least go ask her if she needs some help. Especially since that tired-ass brother of mine won't offer any."

Elijah squeezed Camden's asscheek again, planting a loud smack of a kiss across his lips before sitting up, swinging his legs over the edge of the bed, and heading off to the bathroom.

Camden remained in the bed, intending to get a few more moments of rest before he had to return to the outside world. He'd just found a comfortable position where the mattress was still warm from Elijah's heat when he heard the shower running. The thought of Elijah's satin skin covered in water made his cock twitch. His lips spread wide across his face as he sat up and looked at the closed bathroom door.

"No sense in wasting water with two showers."

He laughed to himself at the ridiculous idea of water conservation being his goal. Camden knew there was only one reason he would slide into the shower with Elijah: whenever Elijah was naked, Camden wanted to be there. It was as simple and hedonistic as that, and Camden had not one bit of shame about it.

It was amazing the change a day made.

ELIJAH was looking in the fridge for something to drink while he waited for Camden to finish up in the bathroom when his burner vibrated again.

"Hello."

"Is he with you?" Her words were rushed, peppered with fear.

"Yeah, what's happened?" Elijah was already walking toward the bathroom door, banging, yelling for Camden to hurry up before she could respond.

"My man on the inside was made. I don't know how, yet. But his body was found under the L train near Livonia and Van Sinderen Avenues. Don't let Camden out of your fucking sight. Where do you have him stashed?"

"At a house in Westchester. I'll text you the info."

"Keep him in that damn house until I get there. I'm on my way."

Elijah grabbed Camden's hand and pulled him through the connecting garage door. Somewhere between the mudroom and the kitchen he gave him the CliffsNotes version of what had transpired along the way. The moment they were inside the kitchen, the lack of the familiar aroma of seasoned meat being fried and then smothered with gravy set his alarms off.

He looked down at his watch and noted he and Camden had spent about three hours enclosed in Elijah's ready-made love shack. By now, the evidence of his mother's culinary mastery should be present.

Elijah heard his father and brother screaming sports terms from the family room. He took Camden by the hand and pulled him along as he walked to the family room.

"Pops, where's Mama?"

Neither his father nor brother turned away from the football game filling the mounted large-screen television. "She went to the store to get some stuff for dinner." His father rattled the words off and returned what little attention he'd spared to Elijah's question back on the game.

"We've got a situation; we need to get her here now. Get her on the phone." Elijah glanced around the room again while his father got his phone out. "Where's Viv?"

His brother pulled his gaze away from the television screen, paused the DVRed game, and answered him. "Downstairs sleeping. What the hell is wrong with you?"

Elijah didn't answer. He just watched as his father made the call, tapping the speaker icon as the line rang.

"Hey, baby." Evelyn's happy voice greeted his father.

"Where you at, Ev?"

"I'm still shopping for dinner."

"Ev, you left here three hours ago. You got Elijah worried. You need to get back to the house."

There was a brief pause before his mother's bubbly voice filled the room again. "Walter, honey, I couldn't find what I needed at the store. Elijah's corner market didn't have those tiny sliced carrots and those white raisins I love so much for the potato salad. I took a cab to that larger natural foods place a little farther out. I should be back soon."

The call ended, and panic settled in the pit of Elijah's stomach as he yanked his burner phone from his pocket.

Camden stepped into the room, placing a comforting hand on Elijah's shoulder. "What's wrong? She's just at the supermarket."

"Camden, you'd see world peace before my mother put unnecessary shit like carrots and raisins in her damn potato salad. That was a code. My mother's in trouble."

Elijah put the phone to his ear, relieved Captain Searlington answered on the first ring.

"What's wrong?"

Elijah had never been more grateful for Captain Searlington's directness, because he didn't have time for pleasantries when his mother was in danger. He let out the shaky breath he'd been holding since he waited the moment before Captain Searlington's voice traveled across the line, then uttered the words no son ever wanted to speak. "The Path has my mother."

ELIJAH'S hand throbbed where his nails cut into his palm as he stood in the middle of his living room watching Captain Searlington and his fellow officers set up command.

This wasn't his first time being part of a missing persons search. He'd watched family members standing around hopelessly as law enforcement set up shop. But in all his years on the force, he'd never surmised that he would be the one waiting while those in charge figured out what to do. No, he didn't do waiting, and the endless sinking feeling in the pit of his stomach as he stood unable to do anything about finding his mother, told Elijah he liked being on the other side of the table much better than his current position.

"Dear God, what have I done?"

The soft sound of Camden's voice pulled Elijah's attention from the unfolding scene and made him focus on Camden. Elijah moved toward him, placing a single finger under Camden's chin, forcing the man to look up to him. "This is not your doing, Cam. This is the work of a madman."

Elijah was technically correct. But as his father, brother, and sister-in-law filed down to the basement together when the police arrived, Elijah couldn't help but wonder if they stepped aside to give his fellow officers the room, or if they blamed him so much for this fiasco that they couldn't stand to be in his presence right now.

Elijah could see doubt cloud Camden's wide eyes. "Elijah, we both know the reason this is happening. There's no place else to lay the blame except for on my shoulders."

Captain Searlington interrupted Elijah's response, calling his name from across the room.

"We're ready." Captain Searlington's voice was steady but direct. She stood with her hands braced on her waist and her legs shoulder-width apart. With her gun holster sitting on her hip, she looked like a fierce superheroine ready to conquer the villains with her superpowers.

The description wasn't far off. There were times this woman had in fact slapped an *S* on her chest and saved the day. For his mother's sake, he hoped this time would be no different.

"They haven't called to notify us of the kidnapping or make any demands. My guess is they're still figuring out how to leverage your mother's capture." Captain Searlington was right. No calls had come in yet. If this were any random snatch and grab, he'd be worried, well, more worried than he already was. But knowing that they'd forced her to give his father that bullshit line about shopping for potato salad ingredients, it inclined him to agree with Captain Searlington. They didn't want them to notice she was gone yet.

"We've got everyone in your family's phone tapped, including your home phone. The Westchester PD are allowing us to take point on this, so we've got boots on the ground canvassing the areas she was last known to be in. Smyth and his team are going through the street cams to see if we can pick up anything that way too. We will find these bastards, Stephenson. We'll get her back."

Elijah believed her. He had to. Thinking of any alternative where his police brethren didn't save his mother wasn't something Elijah could make himself do.

"What do you need me to do, Captain?"

Captain Searlington took a long breath before raising her eyes to his. "Elijah, you know I can't have you involved in this investigation."

His heart beat faster in his chest as he saw resolve settle in Captain Searlington's eyes. "You can't cut me out of this. This is my mother, Cap. Is it because you don't trust me? I know I haven't been in the field for a minute, but I'm still a good cop."

Elijah stiffened as he said the last line, realizing his voice had silenced the entire room, drawing the eyes of the other cops to where he and Captain Searlington stood. He took in a breath, trying his best to ignore the other people standing around them and to focus on his boss. He knew what they all must think. He couldn't protect himself. How could he be trusted to protect someone else?

He couldn't concentrate on their assumptions. Before his attack, he was a good cop. That's all he could think about right now. This was his mother. There was no way he'd fuck this up. He had to be the one to bring these bastards in.

Captain Searlington placed a firm hand on his shoulder before tipping her head toward the doorway. Elijah nodded and followed her out of the family room, down the hall, and to the empty kitchen.

"Elijah, I have no doubts about putting you back on the street. If I did, I would never have assigned the ADA's case to you."

Elijah lifted his brow and crossed his arms over his chest. "I thought you said you assigned me because brass demanded it? That Camden's boss requested it?"

Half of her mouth lifted into a knowing smile. She didn't even have the decency to look apologetic when he caught her in a lie.

"His boss requested it. And I agreed that you would be the best candidate for the job."

Elijah released a rough sigh and let his arms fall to his side. "Why would you do this? Why would you play with Camden's life like that?"

"Elijah. You were jumped by a couple of tweakers. There is no shame in that. I never wanted you anyplace but on the streets, but I knew you had doubts. I figured a job like this one would put you back out in the field in a controlled enough way that you'd realize you still had what it took to make a difference in a job made for you."

Elijah turned away from her and walked over to the island. He wrapped his fingers around the cold granite and squeezed until the hard stone made his fingers ache. The bite of pain took his focus off his anger and kept his mind present in the moment. Otherwise, he might forget the respect and friendship he had for this woman who also was his boss.

"Don't be so fucking proud of yourself when the result of your little game is that my mother is missing."

"Elijah, let's not start with the blame game. I'm not the one who had his entire family involved in what was supposed to be a protective custody detail."

"You blaming me?"

Elijah didn't want to look at her. He was too afraid she'd say what was already rolling around in his head. He closed his eyes, trying hard to pull himself together. He couldn't afford to fall apart now. Not when his mother's life was in the balance.

"Actually, I do. If I'd known your family was here, I probably would've signed off on them being here. It was too dangerous to move Warren. But I would never believe you'd be lax enough to not warn them of the dangers. Why was your mother walking the streets by herself? She was missing for three hours before you figured out that something was wrong. Where were you in that time? Why the fuck didn't you realize what was up before then?"

Elijah swallowed the bitter pill Captain Searlington was shoving down his throat. She asked the same question he would if their roles were reversed, and Elijah knew there was no reasonable answer that would make it all not his fault.

"Officially, I'll take the flack on this one. But we both know this could only happen because your head wasn't in the game. It was on Warren."

He heard her step closer to him, placing a gentle hand on his upper arm when she stood in front of him. "Regardless of whose fault this is, the blame lies solely with the Path. Let's keep it on them, and focus on how to get your mother back. Part of that is letting me and the team handle it. You're too close."

"We may not have any choice in the matter." Lieutenant Bryan Smyth's voice pulled Elijah and Captain Searlington's attention behind them and the ringing phone in Smyth's hand. "Answer it, Elijah. The monitoring is already set up."

Elijah grabbed the phone and answered it with a measured, "Hello."

"We know your cop friends are listening. If you want to see your mother alive again, you're gonna do exactly as I say. It's simple really. Him for her."

Chapter Twenty-Four

"HELL, no!"

Camden shook as Elijah's booming voice filled the room. The sound alone was enough to put his nerves on edge. Knowing Elijah's refusal to go along with his captain's plan could result in Evelyn's death didn't help his situation either.

"Stephenson, we have little choice in the matter. We've got twenty minutes to make it to the drop-off at the I-95/Pelham Parkway intersection. There isn't enough time to scope things out and make a tactical plan to grab your mom. We're working on that now, but until we get the info, we need to come up with a counterplan. We have to at least humor these fools. We have to let them think they're getting what they want."

Elijah pulled his hair into a low-riding ponytail at the base of his neck. It was a sign of stress for Elijah. The minute he became tense about something, he pulled the ever-present hair elastic off his wrist and swept his hair from his face and his shoulders.

Everything in Camden ached to comfort Elijah. Evelyn didn't deserve this, and the stress it was piling on top of Elijah was almost unbearable to witness. Camden folded his arms around himself, trying to quiet the guilty pressure building inside him.

"There's got to be another way, Captain. We can't just trade one for the other. These people are crazy. They put a bomb under his car and nearly killed him. The moment Camden walks on the scene, they will kill him and my mother. You can't think you can trust them to not double-cross us."

"Stephenson, I said nothing about giving Camden to these people. I said we'd let them believe they were getting what they wanted."

"So, you're gonna throw our mama to the wolves to protect Elijah's man?" The room became quiet, and everyone turned to see Emmanuel and the rest of the Stephenson clan standing in the background. They were fortunate the only cops in the room were Elijah, his captain, and Lieutenant Smyth. If anyone else had walked in and heard Emmanuel's proclamation, things would've been so much worse. "That can't be what you're suggesting, is it, Captain Searlington?"

Walter placed a firm hand on Emmanuel's shoulder. "Son, it's not as simple as that. Captain Searlington and the rest of your brother's people are doing the best they can."

Emmanuel shrugged his father's hand from his shoulder and stepped toward Elijah and Captain

Searlington. "The best that they can would be to give these people what they want and save my damn mama instead of protecting Elijah's boyfriend."

"Manny, we're gonna get her back, man. But sacrificing Camden to do that isn't a plan we can agree to. We cannot ask that of Camden."

Camden saw worry and hurt fill Emmanuel's eyes. He hadn't known the man long. He hadn't known any of the Stephensons long, but there was something about this family that made Camden's protective nature flare. Hell, before he'd met these people he hadn't known he had a protective side. But watching them crumble under the threat of losing their matriarch was cutting Camden inside like hot metal through butter.

"What if you weren't asking, Elijah? What if I offered instead?"

Elijah turned to him, shaking his head. "Camden. I love that you would offer, and as tempting as it is, I can't accept it. We do not trade one hostage for another. That is not NYPD policy."

Emmanuel turned to their father, worry and frustration carved into the lines of his face. "You can't agree with them. She's your wife. Do something."

The usual stoic expression Walter Stephenson wore threatened to fall with each tremble of his squared jaw. "Your brother is not wrong, Emmanuel. Everything in me wants to get your mother now. But sacrificing Camden isn't the way we do that. If we do that, they'll both end up dead."

Camden watched as the three Stephenson men each processed those words. Emmanuel spared Camden a sorrowful glance that tore at Camden's heart. This family was falling apart in front of his eyes, and none of them would be all right until they returned Evelyn unharmed.

"Manny." Elijah's voice was thick with emotion as he called his brother's name. He stepped closer to Emmanuel, wrapping his arms around him. "We will find these motherfuckers and end them before they hurt Mama and still protect Camden at the same time."

"I'm scared, E."

Elijah held his brother tighter, wrapping him in a protective cocoon. The sight of the two men clutching at each other for strength while Vivienne walked across the room to embrace their bone-weary father made Camden hurt for this family more.

The notion of feeling so much for a group of people he'd only spent days with seemed strange even to him. But this family had raised a man he cared for. If he cared about Elijah, how could he not be ripped to shreds by watching their pain?

It made little sense, this connection he had with this man and these people. But logical or not, there was something powerful about the Stephensons that had grabbed hold of Camden's heart and wouldn't let go.

We loved each other, so we took care of each other.

Evelyn would be proud that the people she loved most were doing just as she'd expected, taking care of one another no matter how much it hurt. Ache squeezed his heart, and Camden understood why Evelyn's words were so accurate. Watching the man he loved hurt and knowing he couldn't do anything to change it made Camden's chest constrict with the discomfort of helplessness.

But are you really helpless?

As soon as the thought sparked in the back of his mind, Camden resolved to follow it through. Elijah would hate him for it later, but Camden couldn't allow that to keep him from doing what was right.

His eyes looked down on the corner of the counter where Elijah had dropped his keys when they entered through the back door. Camden made a quick swipe of his hand, fisting the keys quietly in his palm. He slipped them into his pocket and glanced back at the scene still unfolding in the middle of the kitchen.

All eyes were still on the Stephensons. Camden took one final glance and slipped out of the back door. He didn't look over his shoulder as he made his way through the backyards of the connecting properties. He just kept going until he found the dark blue sedan Elijah informed him of the night the Stephensons arrived. It wasn't until he was already driving down the block that he allowed himself to glance at the retreating small house through the rearview mirror.

"Please forgive me, Elijah. I couldn't let her die because of me." Camden was doing the wrong thing for the right reason. He just hoped Elijah would understand why.

Chapter Twenty-Five

"I SWEAR to God I'm gonna wring his fucking neck when I catch him."

Elijah took a quick look over to the driver's side of the unmarked sedan where Captain Searlington focused on the road. He wasn't supposed to be in the car with her, but after threatening bodily harm to Smyth if he didn't get out of Elijah's way, his captain reluctantly agreed to let him partner with her instead.

"Not if I catch him first, Cap."

"Right hand to God, I cannot stand rich people."

Elijah glanced at his boss through the narrowed slits of his eyes. "Wait, aren't you married to a rich dude?"

"And your point?"

Elijah threw up his hands and shook his head. Everyone in their right mind knew the captain's husband was off-limits. Elijah would be in enough hot water with Camden running off alone; he didn't want to add to Captain Searlington's bad mood by reminding her that her man and the person who was currently infuriating her were cut from the same cloth.

"Stephenson, how well do you know this man beyond the brief history the DA described to me?"

Elijah kept his eyes fastened to the road, looking for hazards as they sped through the streets with lights and sirens blazing. "I'm not sure what you mean?"

"I've met Camden Warren all of once. He seemed entitled and self-centered. Nothing about him screams sacrificial lamb. What's really going on here?"

Elijah was grateful they'd made it beyond the local streets and onto the highway where there was no intersecting traffic. Trying to explain what occurred between him and Camden was too distracting for him to watch out for oncoming cars and pedestrians in the intersections as his Captain focused on the road ahead of them, and unravel the complicated ball of webbing his feelings for Camden had become.

"As my captain, I don't think you really want to know the answer to that question. This way, you still have plausible deniability."

She nodded, eyes still fixed on the road, and then sped down the left lane of the Hutchinson River Parkway. "In that case, I guess I don't need the specifics. Let me offer you the same advice my captain gave me when I fell in love with someone he assigned me to protect. Tread carefully. Do your damn job and keep this shit as quiet as you can until this case is closed. Because if it gets out you two were together during the case, you'll be the one to suffer, Elijah, not him."

Elijah gave her a silent nod. She wasn't wrong. Camden's name came with clout that Elijah's would never carry. If this shit went sideways, Elijah's career would take the hit, not Camden's.

"Trust me, keeping it quiet isn't an issue at the moment, Cap. It might never be if we don't get there in time."

"We'll get there."

They exited the highway, driving until they hit Pelham Parkway West. As they neared the exchange location, Elijah could see Camden walking away from his vacated vehicle and moving toward the open clearing where another car was parked.

As Elijah caught sight of Camden's intended path, he could see his mother walking from the opposite direction, toward Camden with an armed man pointing a gun in their general direction.

Before Captain Searlington could bring the car to a complete stop, Elijah was jumping out of the vehicle with his weapon drawn as he took cover behind his opened door.

Captain Searlington grabbed her gun and speaker mic before yelling, "NYPD, everybody down on the ground now!"

Elijah's mother turned toward him, but couldn't seem to move. Just beyond her, the gunman turned his aim to Elijah. Camden must have seen her predicament too, because he jumped, pulling Elijah's mother to the ground just as the gunman lined up his shot. As the man opened fire, Elijah and Captain Searlington pulled their triggers too.

He didn't care about policy. This fucker fired a weapon near his mother. There was no coming back from that. He aimed for the kill shot. Captain Searlington must have too, because the end result was two bullets in the head, two in center mass, and several more piercing the car behind the gunman.

While the assailant's lifeless body slumped to the ground, Elijah took aim at the driver in the car.

The driver tried to speed off but was surrounded by several police cars converging from several directions. As other officers came to their aid, securing the scene, Elijah ran directly for the spot next to a large lamppost where Camden and his mother lay in a ball of bodies and limbs.

"Mama, Cam!" Elijah pulled their bodies apart with the help of Captain Searlington. His mother's face was covered with ashen, dried tear stains. Her eyes blinked open as she heard Elijah's voice. "Mama, it's okay. Everything's all right. We got you."

Elijah glanced down at Camden, waiting to see the crystal blue of his eyes shining back at him. Instead, he found Camden's eyes still closed. His jaw was hanging open, and his limbs were limp. "Camden, come on, wake up."

Elijah ran his fingers through Camden's hair, trying to coax him to awaken. He stopped when sticky dampness began to cover his fingers. Cold fear spread through him as frank red blood covered his digits.

"Oh God, no." His words pulled Captain Searlington's attention to Elijah. When understanding registered on her face, she reached over, placing two fingers against Camden's neck, feeling for a pulse.

"Was he hit with a stray, or did he just hit his head on the ground?"

"There's too much blood." Cold fear spread through him as he tried to assess Camden's injury. Bullets pierced different areas of the body in different ways. Depending on caliber, trajectory, and the position of the target, they could look as meaningless as a scratch or as menacing as a gaping hole. All Elijah saw was lots of blood. That alone wasn't a good sign. "I can't tell."

After a few seconds, she pulled her radio from her hip and spoke into it quickly. "This is Captain Heart Searlington of the seven-four. I need a bus for a possible GSW to the head. Victim is a white male, thirty-four, currently unconscious on the scene. Breathing is shallow, heartbeat is thready. Get me that damn bus here now!"

ELIJAH sat in the cold, sterile room, the stench of industrial-strength germicide burning his nasal passage and the back of his throat. He'd like to blame his irritated red eyes on the chemical too, but he knew the swollen rims of his eyes were due to one thing, tears of worry falling faster than he could wipe them away.

Camden hadn't been shot.

Those three words coming from the emergency room attending had loosened the vise around Elijah's heart. For a brief moment relief spread through Elijah as he sent up a grateful prayer of thanks for that extraordinary news. But by the next breath, the doctor had explained the bleeding wound had come from blunt force trauma. Camden had hit his head against a sharp rock on the ground. The force he'd used to drag Elijah's mother down to safety during the shooting turned a simple fall into a significant injury.

Camden hadn't opened his eyes in the five hours since they'd arrived at the hospital. He'd been through the emergency room, to imaging studies, and now he rested quietly inside the small room in the surgical intensive care unit. But after being transported to so many places, Camden remained infuriatingly still.

Thank God for Elijah's badge. He'd never been happier to have the access that his shiny new lieutenant's badge afforded him. The medical staff didn't think twice about violating HIPPA laws whenever they glimpsed that metal emblem of authority hanging around Elijah's neck. His badge also allowed him to follow Camden wherever they moved him with no one looking twice at Elijah.

Once again the job had saved his life. If Elijah had to sit in a waiting room begging for information about a man he had no legal connection to, he would've been in chains for trying to choke someone out by now.

"You can't do this to me, Cam," Elijah leaned down to whisper into Camden's sleeping ear. "You gotta wake up and say something slick that makes me want to curse you out." Elijah wrapped a careful hand around Camden's and squeezed. "I can't take watching you like this. You gotta come back to me, baby. I just found you again. I can't lose you now."

Elijah waited a beat to see if there was any response under Camden's closed eyes, but there was none. His lack of mobility cut through Elijah like a sharp wind, leaving him cold and hollow inside.

Elijah could feel a fresh batch of tears welling up behind his eyes. He wouldn't have bothered trying to keep them in check if he hadn't heard the familiar voices of his boss and her right-hand lieutenant, Bryan Smyth, coming toward the door.

Captain Searlington stepped inside the hospital room first, with Smyth stepping behind her. "Stephenson?"

Elijah wiped his eyes on his T-shirt before he lifted his head to answer her.

"'Sup, Captain?"

"How's Warren doing?"

The uncomfortable fullness of his chest made it difficult for Elijah to breathe. "He banged his head hard when he pushed my mother out of the way." Thinking about the uncertainty of Camden's prognosis ate at Elijah's soul. Elijah was supposed to protect Camden. Instead, Camden sacrificed himself to protect Elijah's mother. It was a debt Elijah could never repay. "The docs say his head CT looks good. No permanent damage. They don't know why Camden is still unconscious. They think it may have something to do with his head taking a hit when his car exploded."

The more he thought about what led to Camden being almost lifeless in that bed, the more his chest hurt. He needed to focus on something else for the time being. "We get anything on the driver?"

Captain Searlington gave a knowing glance to Lieutenant Smyth and returned her gaze to Elijah's. "The driver confessed to everything. He's made a deal with the prosecution. He's got enough info to link all of this back to the Path. They're done. All of their leaders are being picked up as we speak. Edwards' bail has been revoked now that we have him back in custody."

That news should've made Elijah happy. The case was closed. They did their jobs, and the bad guys were going away for a long time. But when he glanced down at Camden's still form, the only thing he could do was hurt.

"How did they find us?"

Smyth stepped closer to the foot of the bed as he opened a folder and laid it on the nearby bedside table. "Gerald Maxwell. Janitor at our precinct for the last five years. Apparently, he joined the Path about a year before when he fell on hard times. They gave him a place to stay and somehow got him the janitorial position at the precinct."

Elijah let his head hang back as he pressed his fingers against his temple. "That bastard saw me walking through the hallway with Camden from your office. How did he find us, though? The house isn't listed under my name. I didn't see a tail, and I took the roundabout way home. What the fuck did I miss?"

Captain Searlington moved closer to him and put a comforting hand on his shoulder. It was odd; Captain Searlington had never been the touchy-feely sort. But there, in her gentle touch, in the softness of her eyes, Elijah sensed understanding and compassion.

"You missed nothing, Stephenson. Your job was to sit on Warren, and you did that. From what we can gather, their plan was to take Warren out when you attempted to move him to court. The fact that Camden never left the house is what kept him alive. They only grabbed Evelyn because she spotted them looking suspicious in their vehicle at the end of the block. They were afraid she'd call the cops. Once they had her, they had to use her." Elijah sent up two silent prayers. The first was for having a garage that attached to his home by a door. If they'd had to walk outside, Camden could've been killed. The second was for his mother's safe return. "They were determined, Elijah. No matter how many of us stood in their way, they would've kept coming."

"She's right, Stephenson," Smyth replied. "Maxwell saw you when you came into the precinct and saw you bring your car around into the underground parking lot. When you came back inside for ADA Warren, he placed a tracer under the tire well on your car while pretending to pick up trash in the parking lot."

Elijah slumped further into the chair at Camden's bedside. Each bit of news should've brought him joy. He'd killed one shooter and his fellow officers apprehended the second. The perp turned witness would now give evidence to help convict the big fish in the Path, and if all things went well, Elijah would probably end up getting a commendation for this. But as he looked at the still body of a man who'd been so full of life while lying in Elijah's arms earlier in the day, the only emotions Elijah could manage were anger, fear, and pain.

"Smyth, would you mind giving us the room for a moment?" Smyth must have agreed because Elijah heard the door slide closed as Smyth exited. "Can we talk for a minute, E?"

Elijah kept his eyes focused on Camden, shrugging briefly before answering her. "Depends on who wants to talk. My captain or my friend?"

His respect for her as his boss notwithstanding, Elijah would not waste a second of his time with Camden discussing policy and procedure. Not when Camden needed him.

It wasn't until he heard her answer, "Heart Searlington, your friend," that he spared her a glance in her direction. "E, this is much more than him being your protectee, isn't it? What happened at your house?"

What indeed? In a handful of days, Elijah had gone from pretending he couldn't care less about Camden to losing his heart.

Elijah shook his head as their days in captivity replayed on a wide-screen in his head. The longing, the laughter, the loving had all consumed Elijah, making him forget to protect himself from Camden and every tempting detail about the man. Yeah, Elijah hadn't lost his heart; he'd willingly given it away.

"You fell in love, didn't you?"

Without hesitation, Elijah nodded his head, communicating the truth, even though he didn't dare speak the words. Those specific words were for Camden. If he couldn't say them to him, he wouldn't share them with anyone else either.

"Take it from someone who fucked around and fell in love with a principal in her case too, you'd better make sure this shit is worth it. Be sure you want to run the distance with it because it could cost you your job."

"Have you ever regretted your decision to choose love over the job, Heart?"

She let out a long breath and pulled up a chair next to Elijah's. "The only regret I have is that I didn't do it sooner. Kenneth has and always will be my everything. Is Camden your everything?"

Elijah let the single tear sliding down his cheek speak for him. It must've been enough, because she nodded and said, "I thought so," as she handed him a facial tissue from the box on the bedside table.

"I got your back, E. Just be careful. This guy's father is the fucking chief judge of the New York Court of Appeals. If this shit goes south, we're both up shit creek."

Elijah cleared his throat before trying to use his vocal cords. His boss's warning didn't go unheard. This situation was bound to get messy for several reasons. His job, Camden's position as the second-in-command at the prosecutor's office, this case, and most probably because of who Camden's father was. In Elijah's mind, it didn't matter how messy things became. Camden was worth it all.

"Speaking of, when will His Honor and his wife arrive?"

"Tomorrow, after he's done with an important case he has to render a decision on in Albany." Heart stood, walking toward the glass door, looking over her shoulder as her hand touched the door handle. "Make use of the time you have. I hear Daddy Dearest is a real piece of work."

Elijah grabbed Camden's limp hand in his, dropping a ghost of a kiss on the back.

"He might be a piece of work, but so am I. I'm not leaving until Camden tells me to."

Chapter Twenty-Six

CAMDEN'S head hurt. He tried to pull himself from the thick haze his mind seemed to be drowning in, but the light bleeding through the murky water of his thoughts appeared too far away for him to reach.

Comforting warmth cupped his cheek, giving him an anchor to grab on to in the vast nothingness of wherever the hell he was right now.

"That's it, baby. Open those pretty blue eyes for me. I've been waiting a long time to see them."

Camden's eyes squeezed tighter against the pain in his head. Was that Elijah's voice, or was Camden conjuring the soul he wanted most by his side at this moment?

The warm hand on his cheek coaxed Camden through what seemed like eternal night, through slivers of light that led him closer and closer to the inviting sound of Elijah's voice.

"'Lijah?"

"So, we're at the nickname stage of this relationship, huh? I mean, most people call me E for short, but I could get used to that."

Camden wanted to laugh, but the throbbing in his head made him think twice about doing something so reckless. He cleared his throat instead and coughed when the dryness tickled it.

Before he could ask, there was a straw at his lips. He leaned his head forward and took several short pulls. Relief flooded him when cool water restored moisture to his mouth, tongue, and throat.

"How long have I been asleep? Why's my head hurt so bad?"

"You arrived in the hospital yesterday. As for the pain in your noggin, that's a long story. Let me get someone in here to tend to your headache."

Camden remained still until Elijah returned with a physician's assistant in tow. The PA introduced herself and then examined him. Shining a godawful penlight in Camden's eyes that mimicked a hot laser slicing through flesh. Once the PA finished poking and prodding Camden and made certain he was oriented to person, place, and time, she scribbled in his chart and promised Camden the nurse would be in to administer pain medication.

A few moments later and the blessing that is pharmaceutical intervention came in the form of two tiny acetaminophen capsules. "How long have I been out?" Camden spared a quick glance at Elijah. In the low lighting of the hospital room, Camden could hardly make out Elijah's features. It didn't matter, though.

He'd memorized the lines and angles of Elijah's unique face years ago.

From hooded lids he could see something akin to fear etching sharp lines under Elijah's cheeks and emphasizing the dark shadows under sunken, tired eyes.

Camden patted the empty space on the bed next to him and gestured for Elijah to sit there. "Come here. Tell me what I missed while—"

"I thought they shot you in the head, Camden. With all the blood on your head, I thought I was going to lose you."

"Elijah…."

Elijah sat next to him, lacing his fingers through Camden's, and held Camden's hand close to his heart. "I couldn't breathe, baby. I couldn't breathe when I saw you slumped over my mother so limp and lifeless."

A flash of the moments leading to his fall brought Evelyn Stephenson to the forefront of his mind. She was afraid, frozen, unable to move to safety on her own. "Your mother, she's all right?"

Camden held his breath as he waited for Elijah's answer. If he'd done anything to harm her, Camden could never forgive himself.

Elijah nodded and kissed Camden's hand. "Because of you, yeah." Camden released the breath he was holding and said a silent prayer of thanks as his heart slowed to a normal pace. "They kept her overnight for observation because of a previous heart attack. She's got a couple of bruises from the fall, but she's otherwise okay. They're releasing her later today."

"Then there's nothing to worry about. We're both fine."

Elijah didn't seem to share Camden's easy assessment of the events. "Things could've ended differently for everyone involved, Cam. I could've lost one or both of you. It made me realize what's important."

Elijah moved closer, touching his forehead to Camden's as he closed his eyes. "You're what's important, Cam."

Camden smiled at the shortening of his name. It wasn't the first time he'd heard Elijah use it, but somehow it was more profound, its significance resting like a comforting weight on Camden's chest. "'Cam'? I guess we really are at the cute name part of our relationship."

Elijah's smile was the only acknowledgment he offered of Camden's observation before he continued. "Having you in my life, creating the relationship we spent the weekend pretending we had, that's what's important to me."

Elijah pressed a sweet kiss across Camden's lips and tightened the grip he had on Camden's hand. "Being with you is all that matters. Loving you is all that matters. I know I was an asshole to you when this case started, but if you give me the smallest chance, I promise—"

Elijah didn't get to finish his sentence before Camden placed his free hand around Elijah's neck and pulled him hard against his lips. Camden didn't know what he'd done to deserve Elijah's affections, but he knew enough to realize he wouldn't turn them away for anything or anyone in the world.

Elijah's lips parted and allowed Camden the access he craved. He was stuck in a hospital bed and nursing the mother of all headaches. But in this moment where Elijah laid bare his soul, Camden would've tolerated any amount of discomfort to be with him like this.

"You never have to apologize for anything that happened between us, then or now. I was the one who fucked it up with my cowardice."

Elijah tried to interject, but every time he attempted to speak, Camden would kiss him. It wasn't the most mature way to deal with the situation, but it worked. Elijah eventually gave up and returned Camden's kisses instead.

"I have spent my entire life living by my father's rules. So afraid of disobeying him I let the best thing that ever happened to me walk away. No more. Leaving you again isn't an option."

Elijah chuckled and stole another kiss from Camden. "Good, because if I have to cuff you to the bed to make certain you stay near, I will."

Camden eased away from Elijah, letting his heavy head fall gingerly against the pillow. "I didn't know bondage was your kink, Lieutenant."

Elijah winked an eye as a broad smile swept across his face. "That's what happens when you don't give a guy the chance to show you more than a night."

Camden raised one hand in the air and placed the other over his heart. "I promise I will never make that mistake again. You're stuck with me."

"Good" was Elijah's only response before he leaned in for another kiss. They were in a hospital room, making out like teenagers, and things had never aligned more perfectly in Camden's life than in this mundane, yet probably inappropriate, moment.

He should probably care about things like the medical staff walking in and witnessing this sweet and playful moment between the two. But somehow, with Elijah's lips touching his, Camden couldn't find a give-a-damn to offer.

"What the hell is going on here?"

Camden swore under his breath. Whoever was interrupting this moment was risking life and limb, even if they didn't know it.

Camden managed to mutter, "Come back later," between the soft presses of his mouth against Elijah's.

"Camden!"

The familiar rigidity in that voice forced a cold chill to travel down Camden's back. He'd heard his name called like that countless times before. That specific mixture of disappointment, shock, and judgment could only be produced by one person.

Camden broke away from the inviting feeling of Elijah's mouth on his and pressed his head against the pillow on the elevated back of the bed.

"Cam, you know this man?" Elijah's voice, full of concern and a hint of protectiveness, warmed Camden's heart as Elijah moved from his perch on the bed and stood up facing their uninvited guests.

"I should say he does. The question, young man, is who are you and why are you mauling my son in his hospital bed?"

SHIT! So, this was the famed Judge Warren. He was every bit the menacing picture everyone warned Elijah of. As tall as both Elijah and Camden, with broad shoulders and an otherwise lean frame. The small-rimmed glasses he wore gave the angles of his face a harsh, authoritative look that probably would've made Elijah piss himself if he hadn't been raised to believe every man was his equal.

"Elijah Stephenson, this is my father, Judge Michael Warren, and my mother, Gertrude Warren." Elijah blinked at the introduction of Camden's mother. The judge sucked up so much attention in the room, Elijah had hardly noticed the small-framed, petite woman who stood next to her husband.

"Mother, Father, this is Lieutenant Elijah Stephenson." Camden snaked his hand around Elijah's and gave it a reassuring squeeze as he looked up at him. "I guess the phrase 'my boyfriend' sounds a little juvenile, considering our ages, but for lack of a better term, that's what he is. He's mine."

The possessiveness that colored Camden's voice made Elijah's chest swell with pride. Hearing Camden claim him in front of the very people whose feared opinions had been the thing to drive him away from Elijah in the first place made any doubt Elijah had that they wouldn't make it dissipate into thin air.

In that moment, Elijah realized he didn't need to be Camden's protector, because Camden was his.

"Obviously your head injury is more significant than the doctors diagnosed," Mrs. Warren huffed, passing a dismissive, gloved hand in the air. "You can't just claim strange men as your love interest, Camden."

"He's not a stranger, Mother. I've known him for five years."

Elijah almost laughed out loud at the secret glances passing between both of Camden's parents. Their unspoken displeasure was painted across their stiff faces in bold colors.

"Mr. Stephenson, is it?" Camden's father's tone was condescending at best, outright rude at its worst.

"Lieutenant Stephenson, NYPD," Elijah corrected him. The badge hanging from his neck should've been enough to show his rank. But Elijah didn't like people who tried to belittle others, just because they were too busy being impressed with their own titles. This man might have more money than Elijah ever would, but he wouldn't disrespect his badge, even if he was a fancy-ass judge.

"Lieutenant, then. Would you mind leaving us alone to visit with our son?"

"Sir, no disrespect—"

Camden placed a firm hand on Elijah's forearm, drawing his attention away from the judge. "It's all right, Elijah. I need to talk to my parents."

"You sure?" Elijah removed his arm from Camden's grasp to run his fingers through Camden's hair. "You don't have to do this alone, Cam. Never again." Elijah wasn't certain what the deal was between Camden and the judge, but his protective instincts flared in front of the man.

"It's fine, Elijah."

There was pleading in his voice that made Elijah relent. As much as he wanted to protect Camden, especially from this man whose very presence seemed to suck the joy out of the room, Camden had to fight his own battles if he were ever to break free of his father's hold.

Elijah nodded. "I have to check in on my mom. Her discharge papers should be ready by now. Once I have her settled at home, and I change my clothes—" Elijah leaned down to kiss Camden before facing the judge. "—I'll be right back."

In his peripheral vision, Elijah could see Camden's mother nervously playing with the cuffs of her jacket as she stood off to the side. The judge, however, didn't blink. He stood silent, watching as Elijah made his way to the door.

Once through the doorway, Elijah kept walking until he was standing in front of the elevator. He gave a hard two-fingered punch to the Down button twice. He recalled his boss's words with extreme clarity and repeated them when the elevator dinged and the doors slid open.

"Right hand to God, I cannot stand rich people."

"CAMDEN, what the hell do you think you're doing?"

"I'm fine, Father. Thanks for asking."

"Don't be a smartass, Camden. You kissed that man in the open where anyone could see. Are you determined to ruin your chances for running for public office?"

Camden rested his head against his pillows and rubbed his temple. He'd been in his father's presence all of five minutes, and already the pain slicing through his head was doing its best to return.

"I fail to see how kissing someone I care deeply about will negatively impact my ability to run for office. He's a decorated police officer, for God's sake, Father. You can't get better PR than that."

"Camden, we've been over this. Marrying the right man will secure your political future. We agreed the senator's son was the best candidate for the job."

"You agreed, Father."

"Camden, don't speak to your father that way. He's only trying to do what's best for you."

Camden closed his eyes and took a deep breath. He was used to his mother agreeing with whatever mandate his father issued. It was probably the reason they'd been married for over forty years. She backed Judge Warren no matter how insane his schemes for power were. What Camden wouldn't give for her to have ever supported him with the same ferocity.

The memory of Elijah standing here only moments before ready to stand at his side, to put himself in between the threat he perceived from Camden's father, made joy bloom inside him. His unanswered longing for his mother to take his side once was gone. He had Elijah's love now. That was enough.

"What is best for you is to marry someone with the same standing in the world. As lovely as I'm certain this young man is, he can't turn an election in your favor, Camden. I won't allow it."

This was the part in the story where Camden always acquiesced, giving his father whatever he was demanding at the moment just so he wouldn't have to face his father's wrath and disappointment.

But those days were over. He'd faced the worst yesterday and he'd survived. His father's disappointment didn't even come close to the things he was afraid of anymore. Now that he had Elijah, the only thing he feared was losing him.

"You won't allow it?" Camden snapped.

His father stood taller, folding his arms over his chest to assert his authority in the room.

After sitting on the bench for most of Camden's life, Michael Warren accepted that his word was the literal law. Being challenged wasn't something his father was used to. And if the involuntary tick visible at the base of his father's jaw was a sign, Camden suspected he wasn't too thrilled with being defied now.

"I love him, Father. I will not give him up again for you or your political aspirations for my career. Leave us alone. My relationship with Elijah is not up for discussion."

His mother moved closer to him, placing a gentle hand on his shoulder. "Camden, you're obviously not feeling like yourself. Maybe you should rest before making any rash decisions."

"Stop babying the boy, Gertrude. If he thinks he's man enough to make his own decisions, let him."

His father placed both his hands on the footboard of the bed, his knuckles blanching white as he tightened his hold. "You want to make your own choices, fine. You'd just better be ready to live with the consequences."

His father released the footboard and walked toward the door, glancing over his shoulder at Camden's mother. "Come, Gertrude; it's obvious we're not needed here."

His mother followed behind his father as she always did, leaving him alone in the room. He should have been relieved to be rid of his father's judgmental gaze and his overbearing need to plan every detail of Camden's life. But sitting there alone in his room, the only thing he could feel was dread.

Chapter Twenty-Seven

"CAM, baby, you're supposed to be resting."

Camden didn't bother to respond to that comment. Since they'd exchanged test results last night, Camden's enthusiasm to experience Elijah in all ways with no barriers between them had given him many naughty motivations.

His lips met the hand he currently had wrapped at the base of Elijah's cock, and Camden released a moan filled with equal parts pleasure and amusement. The truth was with his mouth currently filled with Elijah's cock, he couldn't do more than make unintelligible sounds if he wanted to. From Camden's perspective, the wasted energy he'd use trying to explain why Elijah's concerns were baseless would be better spent trying to give him the best blow job of his life.

Elijah's hips moved in an erratic rhythm, attempting to both chase and retreat from Camden's ministrations. If Camden needed any indicators he was good at putting his mouth to work, Elijah's body language told him everything he needed to know.

Elijah's fingers were curled in Camden's hair, tugging in an almost painful grip as Camden's mouth slid down the impressive length and girth, swallowing the tip in the back of his throat.

Elijah's body tensed beneath Camden's, his body racked with powerful spasms. He swallowed once more, working the muscles in his throat, demanding Elijah's surrender to his touch.

Within seconds, Elijah relented and flooded Camden's mouth with his essence. Camden drank with enthusiastic pulls of his cheeks, determined to drain Elijah of every drop of his cum.

As Elijah's body went limp underneath him, Camden heard Elijah's breath audibly catch as Camden used his tongue to swipe at an errant drop hanging perilously from his bottom lip. The man had just spent moments before, but the hunger that rose in the depths of his coal eyes made Camden shiver with need.

"I swear to God, if I were closer to twenty than forty, your ass would be in so much trouble."

Camden's lips bent into a knowing smile. Even though Elijah was closer to forty, his lovemaking always left Camden tender and exhausted in the best of ways. "I'd do my best to explore that theory at length, but I need to go home and get work clothes. The doctor signed off on my return. It's time for me to finish this business with the Path so we can move on with our lives."

He turned to sit up and get out of the bed, but Elijah's hand on his back stopped him. "I know you don't think you're leaving this apartment until I return the favor."

"I can finish in the shower. Just catch a nap before you have to check on your mother."

The word "Nope" coming from Elijah's mouth was the only warning Camden had before he found himself on his back underneath him.

Camden chuckled as he squirmed beneath Elijah, loving the feeling of his smooth skin warming Camden's body in all the right places. "I can see there will be lots of late starts to our mornings together."

Elijah nodded, his long locs cascading over his face and shoulders, teasing the skin on Camden's chest. "You'd better believe it, Mr. Executive Assistant District Attorney. Something we're gonna have to work on if I'm punching a clock at the precinct instead of working cases in the field."

Camden tucked Elijah's hair behind his ear, then cupped a careful hand to his cheek. "You're still taking the cybercrimes position? I thought you'd want to go back to the field?"

Still smiling, Elijah shook his head as he spoke. "There was a part of me that wanted to go back to busting heads and being a hero. I've done that for fourteen years. It's second nature to me. But then I thought about how little I've seen my family over the years. The inconsistencies in my schedule have caused me to miss a lot of important moments. Now that you're here with me, I've decided I don't want to miss any more."

Tightness bloomed in his chest at Elijah's admission. His entire life had been built around someone else's needs and desires. But now, he'd stumbled upon someone who would willingly rearrange his life for no other reason than he wanted to make time for Camden.

Too emotional to speak, he pulled Elijah to him and held him close. And if he had his way, he'd keep him close for the rest of his life.

CAMDEN stepped outside of Elijah's Brooklyn apartment and smiled. He'd started his day an hour later than he'd intended, but after a pair of delightful orgasms, Camden wasn't all that concerned with keeping his schedule.

The gentle vibrations coming from the back pocket of his jeans made him stand still.

"Camden Warren, how may I help you?"

"Executive ADA Warren, this is Captain Heart Searlington of the seventy-fourth precinct. I was hoping to speak with you today. Would you drop into my office for a few moments?"

Camden glanced at his watch and shrugged. It wasn't as if his and Elijah's early-morning sexy shenanigans hadn't already blown his schedule to hell. Why not make a detour on his way home?

"Sure, I'm close by. I'll see you in ten minutes. Does that work?"

"Outstanding. See you soon."

Camden made the short drive to the precinct and was quickly escorted to Heart Searlington's office once inside. He was about to open the door, but then he heard mention of Elijah's name.

"This could end Stephenson's career, Searlington. If this gets out, the department will not back him."

Panic rose in Camden's throat, driving him to swallow forcefully to move the lump blocking his airway. What the hell could've threatened Elijah's career?

"I promise I'll handle it, Inspector Abrams."

At the sound of feet moving toward the door, Camden sat in a nearby chair, pulled his phone from his back pocket, and pretended to stare at it when Heart opened the door, letting the man he presumed was the "inspector" she'd mentioned earlier exit her office.

"Oh great, you're here."

He nodded in response to Captain Searlington and followed her into her office, then took a seat in front of her.

"Okay, I'm gonna get straight to the point. I told Elijah to be careful of fucking around with you. It's nothing personal, but he stands to lose more than you if this shit goes bad."

The brashness of the captain's speech and tone took Camden aback. "I'm sorry," Camden replied, "I wasn't aware that either of us should give a damn about what you or anyone else thought of our relationship."

To her credit, the woman didn't seem the slightest bit concerned by Camden's flippant tone. "Normally I'd agree with you. But as I understand it, most of your relationship occurred while you were placed in Lieutenant Stephenson's protective custody, making it my business if you were fucking on the department's dime."

"What is this all about, Captain? I would hope you didn't interrupt my plans for today just to ask me if Elijah and I were sleeping together while I was at his house."

He watched her close the folder on her desk and slide it to the edge in front of him. "This is why I called you down here, Mr. Warren."

He picked up the folder and read its contents. It was an official departmental complaint sworn out against Elijah. The complainant accused Elijah of negligent behavior during Camden's case that bordered on the criminal, with terms like "sexual deviance" thrown in for good measure. Whoever drafted this also insisted Elijah be relieved of his duties because of his inability to perform in a professional and dignified manner.

Camden closed his eyes before he read the signature at the bottom of the affidavit. He didn't need to see it to know who wrote this, but in his soul, he prayed his assumption was wrong.

But sadly, when he gathered up enough courage to look down at the document again, he saw his father's distinctive "Honorable Michael C. Warren, JD" scribbled across the signature line.

"My inspector is giving me time to get ahead of this. However, your father is a judge. He can't sit on this forever. Can you talk to your father? Can you get him to rescind this? If he can prove any of this, it could be terrible for Elijah."

Camden slouched back into his chair and released a heavy breath. "What happens between now and when the time your inspector gave you is up?"

"I know I'm crossing a line, but I wanted to let you know what was going on first. If I'd told Elijah about this first, he would've quit and probably never told you why."

He nodded his head. She wasn't wrong. Elijah wouldn't have allowed anyone to back him into a corner. If only Camden had that kind of resolve. Instead, he sat there trembling for no other reason than he knew his father had made a power move and Camden wasn't sure how to get around it.

"I'll talk to my father. This has to be a misunderstanding."

The captain nodded her head. "If I don't hear from you by tomorrow morning, I'll have no choice but to notify Stephenson of this officially. By chance, do you have any experience with representing anyone in IA matters? Because if your father is coming after my lieutenant like this, his PBA rep may not cut it."

Camden stood up, his lawyer game-face settling over his features. "I'm sure my boss would see it as a conflict of interest, but whether it's me, or one of my colleagues, Elijah will have everything he needs to win in court."

The captain shook her head, sadness adding creases to the worry lines taking up residence on her face. "Counselor, we both know whether this goes to court is immaterial. In court your father knows he'd lose. This is about ruining Elijah's reputation, stripping him of his ability to succeed in a job he loves. Once this is officially filed, whether the allegations are founded, Elijah will never make rank again."

Camden shuddered. Elijah had become a cop to follow in his father's footsteps, but he'd succeeded in the department under his own steam. That he could lose it all because of Camden's megalomaniac father was something Camden couldn't allow.

"I promise I'll handle it." He left the captain's office, heading directly for his car in the parking lot. As soon as he closed the driver's door, his phone was out, and he was calling his father's cell phone.

The judge picked up on the first ring as if he was expecting Camden's call. Knowing how strategic that son of a bitch was, Camden didn't doubt he was.

"Why did you do it?"

"Ah, Camden," the judge uttered. His voice was tinged with knowing delight, smugness traveling across the line, making Camden grateful he wasn't close enough to string his father up by his designer tie. "If you're referring to the complaint I swore out against Lieutenant Stephenson, then my answer is that you left me no choice. You wouldn't listen to reason. As your father I had to do what was best for my son."

"How did you even find out Elijah was assigned to this case? None of those details have been released yet."

"I've been on the bench in the highest court of the state for more than a decade. Does it really seem like police files are something I couldn't get my hands on? You're losing your edge, Camden. You of all people should know who I am, and how far I can extend my reach."

Camden's pulse sped up. "You made it sound like Elijah used his badge to coerce me into sex. Nothing like that happened, and you couldn't prove it even if it did. You are trading on other people's pain, Father. Not to mention, you're lying. Everything that happened between Elijah and me has always been consensual."

"That's not my interpretation of it, son. I asked you to stop seeing that man for your own benefit. You wouldn't, so I had to intervene."

Camden wrapped one hand tightly around the steering wheel and squeezed. It was that or punch his hand through the window. The gall of his father to do something like this and name fatherly love as his motivation…. It was infuriating.

"Me leaving Elijah is not an option. I won't walk away from him to please you. I love him."

"Do you love his family also? His father is retired, but his mother still works. Isn't she a nursing director at the county hospital? It would be so sad if negative press about her son led to an unfavorable light being cast on her too. It would be equally shameful if perhaps her superiors discovered something unsavory about her work ethic as well? And what about his brother—"

Camden slapped the heel of his hand against the steering wheel and prayed the distraction was enough to keep him from executing the patricidal thoughts currently swirling around in his head.

"You wouldn't—"

"Camden, you've seen what happens when I'm determined to bring someone down. Are you willing to test the theory that this so-called love of yours will succeed? The truth is, when I'm done with your lieutenant and his family, he will hate you for coming into his life."

Camden closed his fists, letting the nails embed themselves in his skin. His father was ruthless, and he would keep coming after the Stephensons until Camden caved or Elijah pushed Camden away. Either way Camden had no more moves on the chessboard.

With hot tears sliding down his skin, Camden took the only avenue he could. "Drop the complaint and leave Elijah and his family alone, and I'll do what you want."

"See? That wasn't difficult at all. Was it?"

Difficult? Why would torching Camden's only chance at happiness be difficult? Especially when he'd spent years having his free will trampled upon by his father. No, pain and frustration were old friends to Camden by now.

Camden hung up the phone without saying a proper goodbye, tapping on Elijah's icon in his phone's contacts with more force than necessary. He believed in delivering bad news immediately. Better to rip off the bandage and let the healing begin quickly.

When Elijah's jubilant tone greeted him, his stomach sank, and part of him wanted to put this off until another day. But the memory of the complaint he'd read reminded Camden Elijah and his family didn't have another day. He needed to protect them now.

"Elijah, we need to talk."

Chapter Twenty-Eight

ELIJAH sat in the courtroom gallery, with his hands balled into fists on his lap to keep his anger from making him do something stupid like snatching Camden by the back of his neck and dragging him to a dark corner where Elijah could shake some sense into him.

Only days ago, they'd been locked up in Elijah's apartment, loving on each other and making plans for their future while Camden recuperated. But less than an hour after Camden left him to make a clothes run, Camden was on the phone, ending things with him as if it was the most normal thing in the world.

This smelled of that fucking judge. Elijah knew it, and if he could get Camden to talk to him, Elijah was certain he could understand all this and fix things so he and Camden could get back to the loving part of the agenda.

The most Elijah could piece together was Camden had stopped at his precinct. Camden wouldn't tell him why, and neither would Captain Searlington. Both cited tying up loose ends for the case or some such bullshit as a reason for the meeting.

The hair on the back of his neck prickled his skin, telling him they were both lying to him. There was something dirty going on; the intuitive investigator in him was sure of it. And since neither of them wanted to come clean, Elijah would go on the hunt until he had every bit of information he needed to figure out why Camden left, taking Elijah's heart with him.

"Don't do anything stupid, Stephenson."

Elijah swallowed before turning to Captain Searlington and leveling a cold glare in her direction. She might be his superior, but he still wasn't entertaining her input outside of the job since things had fallen to pieces with Camden. He knew Heart usually had his back, but she was holding out on him regarding whatever transpired in her office with Camden. That put her firmly in Elijah's not-to-be-fucked-with category for now.

"I don't think I know what you're talking about, Captain. I'm sitting here enjoying the show like everyone else."

Her narrowed eyes implied she didn't believe him at all. There wasn't much of a show to see. The lawyers had each submitted their documents; the witness was returned to her life, the accepted plea making her testimony unnecessary. All that remained was for the mighty man who ran the Path to say, "I did it, and this is how I did it," for this to all be over.

It didn't matter she knew he was bullshitting. Until she told him the truth, it was business as usual with his boss.

Lee Edwards stood silently until his attorney directed him to speak. The questions issued by the judge were usually closed-ended requiring a "yes" or "no" in response. When the judge asked Edwards why he'd committed such atrocities, he said simply, "Because God predestined me to be Him on earth. It was my sacred duty to burn this sinful world to the ground and recreate it in Our image."

There was no remorse in the cold sound of his voice. His words were exact, leaving no room for interpretation. The man wasn't just evil; he was certifiable.

The judge wasted no time moving to the sentencing portion of the hearing. As the DA explained to Elijah and his family, the prosecution threatened to treat the Path as an organized crime family to get Lee to accept the deal. A RICO charge by the Feds would yield him a needle in his arm; Edwards agreed to plead guilty to all charges for life in a maximum-security prison.

Camden was safe. As much as his most recent antics kept Elijah twisted in knots of angry frustration, the relief of knowing Edwards and his crazy-ass followers couldn't get to Camden anymore gave Elijah peace.

The banging of the judge's gavel pulled Elijah out of his thoughts long enough for him to watch Camden attempt to escape from the courtroom.

Elijah could see how hard Camden tried not to look in Elijah's direction, but one glance was all it took for him to see the mutual ache in Camden's eyes. The pain etched on his face, dark circles under his eyes, the droop in his shoulders—all screamed that Camden hurt as much as Elijah did. Ready to stop the ache, Elijah stepped toward Camden. He avoided Elijah, losing himself in the crowd.

He pushed through a few reporters to glimpse Camden going into a bathroom down the corridor. Elijah took a quick sweep inside the busy area, watching people buzz around the halls, none of them focused on Elijah or what he was planning. One more pass of his gaze over the hall, and he crossed through the throng of people and slipped inside.

He was quiet when he stepped in. So quiet, Camden didn't hear Elijah's entry as he stood, leaning over the sink, washing his face in the running water. Elijah gave a quick glance under the two stalls in the small room before he made his presence known. As far as he could tell, they were alone, and the only way Camden could exit would be to walk through him.

He turned the lock to the closed position, letting it click loudly to draw Camden's attention. When Camden realized he was no longer alone, he snapped his head up. His face was wet, but the red rim around his eyes told Elijah the fresh water tracks weren't entirely due to the stream coming from the sink's faucet.

"Baby, if it feels this bad, why are you doing it?"

Camden returned his gaze to the sink, placing his hand on the countertop to brace himself. He looked so frail, so somber, as if he'd lost the thing that made the bright, fun part of him wither away.

"Elijah, why are you here?"

"It's where I need to be. Baby, what the hell are you doing to yourself?" Elijah stepped closer to Camden, the need to pull him into his arms building in the pit of his stomach as he closed the distance between them.

"Cam, let me fix this. Tell me what's wrong, and I will make it better. I promise you."

Camden shook his head, and a small gasp escaped his lips. The sound was a cross between a whimper and a shriek of pain. It rattled inside Elijah's hollow heart, making its sound reverberate, each echo slicing away at another piece of him.

Camden backed himself against the wall, trying to keep a respectable distance between the two. It might have worked, too, if Elijah cared anything about respectability. Hell, he'd locked them in a courthouse bathroom. All concerns about appropriate ways to handle relationship problems pretty much went out the window at this point.

Elijah stepped closer, placing his hands against the wall on either side of Camden, caging him in, forcing him to look Elijah in the eye.

"I told you I loved you. You said the same to me. You told me you'd never run again, and I believed you. The first time we're more than five minutes away from each other, you call me with some bullshit line about moving too fast."

Camden slowly moved his head from side to side. "Elijah, please, just let this go."

Elijah pressed closer, so close not even light could pass between their bodies. "Tell me what happened, Cam." Elijah moved his mouth to Camden's ear, letting his tongue touch the outer rim, sliding down until it ghosted over Camden's earlobe. Camden trembled beneath him, and he knew their connection wasn't lost. Everything that tied him to this man was still present, a living thing binding them together. And Elijah had no intention of letting it die.

"Just tell me what happened so I can make it better, Camden. So we can get back to who we're supposed to be. I know this isn't you; this isn't us."

Camden's knees shook. Elijah's hand was around his waist, pressing them closer, until Elijah could feel the stiffened flesh of Camden's cock pressing against his.

Elijah nipped at Camden's ear and delighted in the shivers moving through the man's body. He continued to place small bites down Camden's jaw and down the curve of his neck, all the while keeping Camden pressed so tightly against him he could feel the throb of Camden's heartbeat against his chest.

"This was your father, wasn't it?"

Camden went rigid in his arms and not in a good way. Camden tried to push Elijah away, but he refused to budge. Elijah was already halfway convinced Camden's father had somehow made this silly-ass breakup happen. But the way Camden's body was so stiff under his touch, Elijah had no doubt.

He swallowed, trying to keep his temper under control, but knowing the fucking smug bastard was somehow responsible for this made Elijah's blood bubble with rage.

"Tell me." He spoke those two words with quiet strength through clenched teeth. Camden's eyes moved quickly, assessing Elijah's features. He must've seen that Elijah wouldn't be swayed, so he took a steadying breath before he spoke instead.

"I'm trying to protect you, Elijah. He will destroy you."

"I don't give a fuck about what your power-hungry father does to me. As long as we're together, nothing else matters."

Camden's mouth trembled, and his blue eyes shone with unshed tears. "It's not just you. He'll destroy all of you."

Elijah's eyes narrowed as he sought to make sense of what Camden was saying.

"Elijah, he filled out an official complaint against you for misconduct. He made it seem as if you used your influence as my assigned protector to coerce me into bed. I told him we'd fight it. He said we could. But when he was through with that complaint, he'd do the same to your mother and brother. He would come after your entire family if I didn't agree to marry his handpicked candidate."

Elijah stepped back, releasing Camden, moving across the room to slap his hand against the opposite wall. "Son of a bitch! He threatened my family? I don't give a fuck who he is or what title he carries, I will stomp his ass into the ground about my damn mama."

"He's banking on that. I'm trying to prevent that. Please, just let me go, and your family will be safe."

The pleading in Camden's voice broke through his anger and sat in the middle of Elijah's chest, making it difficult to breathe. He let his head hang down for a minute as he pulled himself together before he faced Camden again.

"Your father wants us broken, Camden. When we're apart, we're weak. Don't let your father do this."

"I don't see where I have much choice, Elijah."

Elijah balled his hands into fists, looking up to the ceiling, blowing a long breath through pursed lips. "So, you will make decisions for my life the way your father makes decisions for yours?" He gathered himself enough to risk looking at Camden again. "I'm not about being controlled by anyone, Camden. I want to be with you, and I don't care what anyone else, including your father, my boss, or my boss's bosses have to say about it. I love being a cop, but it doesn't compare to what I feel for you. I love you. My choice will always be you. But maybe I'm the only one feeling that way since running away is always your choice when it comes to me, to us?"

"Don't." There was a flash of fire in Camden's eyes when he said the word. "Sacrifice and running are not the same thing. I'm trying to protect you, Elijah. I don't care about what happens to me. I don't care about my suffering. I don't want to see you hurt, not because you love me." He leaned against the wall again, as if that last outburst had taken more energy, more strength, than he had to give.

"I hurt when you hurt. That's why it nearly killed me when you were in the hospital holding on to life. That's why I tried to trade my life for your mother's. I knew I couldn't watch you suffer if you lost her because of me. It would have killed me. I cannot watch you hurt, Elijah. You losing your job over this bullshit with my father would hurt you. Don't you see? This is the only way I can protect you, all of you."

Elijah smiled as he listened to that last sentence. Camden may not have realized what he'd done, but Elijah did. Camden had admitted to loving his family. As far as Elijah was concerned, that's all the proof he needed to believe in their future together.

"I love you, Cam, and you love me. That's the only thing I'm willing to acknowledge. Being together is the only choice I'm willing to make. If you're ready to make your own decisions, I'll be at my parents' house visiting with the fam. I'm sure with the five of us together, someone is gonna want to get a game of

Spades going. It would be nice to have my partner there with me. We've proven it several times over. We're unstoppable together."

Elijah stepped forward, placing both hands on Camden's face, gently cupping his cheeks as he wiped away the tracks of Camden's fallen tears. "I love you, and my family loves you because I love you. You are mine, and therefore theirs. If you come for one Stephenson, you come for us all. Come to us, let us help you figure out a way to stop this. Don't do this alone."

Elijah touched his forehead to Camden's. It was a way of connecting, as if their minds and hearts melded into one when they touched like this. "We'll be waiting for you. The choice is yours."

Chapter Twenty-Nine

"HE knows the truth."

Camden sat in Captain Heart Searlington's office once again. This was the third time since all of this nonsense began, and he was no less pissed this time around.

"You finally told him about your father's complaint?"

Camden nodded. "You sound as if you'd expected me to do so earlier."

Captain Searlington stood up and walked around to the front of her desk, taking a seat on its edge in front of Camden. "Of course, I did. You two are a couple. Why wouldn't you discuss this and come up with a plan?"

Camden's gaze fell to the floor. Apparently everyone else in the world knew how people who loved each other were supposed to behave in crises.

"I have little experience with relationships, I'm afraid." He cleared his throat before meeting her gaze again. "I assume that ridiculously large wedding set on your finger means you're an expert, Captain?"

She wiggled her marriage finger, admiring the rings Camden mentioned. If his experience in expensive baubles was accurate, whoever placed those rings on her finger had paid a handsome price for them.

"My husband comes from a world like yours. Old money, family business, overbearing parent who thinks they can rule the world through you. The only difference is, his dad and his godfather taught him the strength of family. I knew what it meant to have a strong family, but I didn't truly understand how to tap into that until I met my husband. If you're hiding things like your father's complaint from Elijah, it means you don't understand he's supposed to be the source of your power. It took me a long time to realize my husband, Kenneth, was my center."

Camden leaned back into his chair, still weary from the earlier emotional exchange with Elijah. "What do you advise I do, Captain? My father will use every bit of influence he has to destroy Elijah and his family. How do I fight that?"

"Camden, from what I understand, you're an impressive lawyer. What would you advise someone to do if they were being blackmailed?"

Camden closed his eyes to process her question. He hadn't thought about his father's actions as blackmail before. But what else could they be? The judge had been pulling this for years, demanding Camden behave in a particular manner and throwing the precise penalty at him that would threaten the thing Camden loved most.

"I'd tell them to expose their blackmailers."

She crossed her ankles and offered him a comforting smile. "If you expose your own truth, how can anyone else hold it over your head?"

Camden pulled his cell phone from his jacket pocket. "Have you got any immediate plans over the next hour or so?"

She shook her head. "No. Why?"

Camden smiled as he dialed, waiting for the line to connect on the other end. "Because I was hoping you'd give me a hand in telling my truth."

She clapped her hands together and rubbed them in a conspiratorial manner, smiling as she answered, "What the hell. It's been a minute since I risked my career just to stick it to someone above my pay grade. I'm in."

ELIJAH plated the various meats he'd grilled to perfection on his father's old-school drum grill. It may not be the latest in grilling technology, but that bad boy smoked meat like nobody's business. If his dad left him nothing else but his grill in his will, Elijah would be a satisfied man. Well, mostly satisfied.

He stopped what he was doing to think about Camden. It had been hours since Elijah had coaxed the truth out of him in that bathroom. He'd expected to hear something from him by now. His heart too full of love to let hope completely die, he continued to busy himself with prepping the food while his family played cards inside the house.

It wasn't summer; the hot days had turned to a crisp breeze. It wasn't cold enough for a jacket, but standing out here grilling was probably a testament to the instability of his thoughts. *No time to worry about that. You've got meat to grill.*

He flipped the last of the jerk chicken, brushed more sauce on it, then flipped it again, enjoying the sizzling sound of wet meat being seared by hot metal.

"A-yo, E, come inside," Emmanuel yelled from the back window. If Elijah were home on his quiet block in Westchester, he would've been telling Emmanuel to shut his big mouth. But here, on the block he'd grown up on in East New York, Brooklyn, that familiar "A-yo" coasting across the air to greet him was a soothing balm to his tattered soul. "Your boss and your boy are on the news."

"Camden?"

"You got another man you smashing right now?"

Elijah rolled his eyes and shook his head. His brother's crudeness was also something that was familiar. Too bad that particular trait didn't make him feel as warm and fuzzy as his prior greeting had. He waved Emmanuel off, pulled the remaining food from the grill, and brought two heaping plates full of grilled food into the house.

He made a quick stop at the kitchen counter to make sure the plates were secured, and then he rushed into the family room where his parents, brother, and sister-in-law were sitting with their eyes focused on the television. Elijah sat on the arm of his mother's armchair and joined the viewing. As the commercial ended and the nightly news theme played, a picture of Camden, Heart, and the anchorwoman came into view.

What the hell are you up to, Camden?

"WELCOME to the *News at Six* with me, Marie Jennings. This week the good guys checked a mark in the win column by convicting the leaders of the notorious cult, the Path to Unity. Earlier today I was granted this exclusive interview with two key members of the task force who accomplished this feat. Discover how a joint operation between the Brooklyn District Attorney's office and the seventy-fourth precinct made our streets safer as we roll tape."

Camden swallowed, then patted a dry handkerchief across his brow as he listened to Marie Jennings shoot the interview promo. In a few seconds, they'd be filming again, and it would be time for him and Heart to put his plan into motion.

"Executive Assistant District Attorney Camden Warren and Captain Heart Searlington. The two of you were directly responsible for the capture and conviction of the now defunct Path to Unity, and their leader, Lee Edwards. How did you two accomplish that?"

Camden cleared his throat before he spoke. He'd called his mother and Evelyn shortly before they filmed to make certain his father and Elijah were watching this interview when it broadcast. He *wanted* his father to see this broadcast, but he *needed* Elijah to see it. "It was definitely a joint venture. After the Path bombed my car, Captain Searlington did her best to impress upon me how important it was for me to allow the NYPD to protect me. I understood her, and she was absolutely right, but I wasn't willing to walk away from this trial and let the Path win. So, I refused to go into protective custody."

"It sounds like he wasn't easy to convince, Captain Searlington."

Heart gave a barely there smile, which made Camden's lips curve into a full-on grin. "ADA Warren was difficult to convince. No matter what I told him, how I tried to scare him, he didn't listen. So I brought in my lieutenant, Stephenson, to talk some sense into him."

"Why was Lieutenant Stephenson successful where the captain wasn't, ADA Warren?"

Because he kisses me breathless and fucks me stupid. That was certainly the truth, but Camden was sure getting the show censured by the FCC was probably not a good thing if his plan would work. "Well—" Camden held the breath sitting inside his chest. This was the moment of truth, and if he botched it up, he'd have so much more to lose than a career. "—he's the man I love, so his words weighed a bit more than Captain Searlington's."

"Wait, the man you love? You're romantically involved with the lieutenant?"

"Yes." Camden looked directly into the camera as he spoke. "I've loved him since our first date five years ago, and no matter how much time has passed, that feeling has never waned. It's powerful, it's mutual, and the love we share gets through my stubborn defenses when nothing else will. He told me he was scared for me. That was enough to make me listen to the captain with one caveat. I still refused to allow her to put me in protective custody, but I agreed to get out of the city with Elijah while she and her team worked the bombing case. I strongly believed no one else would protect me the way he would."

The reporter placed her hand over her heart, giving Camden the sweetest fake smile he'd ever seen. "You apparently were right. Can you share with us how he did that?"

Heart placed a hand on Camden's arm to let him know she would take the lead on the last question. "The NYPD obviously can't reveal all of its tactical secrets, but Lieutenant Stephenson is a fourteen-year decorated officer who has always had a gift for strategic takedowns of suspects and criminal organizations. As his captain, I am proud that he represents the best of what NYPD offers."

"Wow, that is remarkable," the reporter responded. "Who would've thought love would literally save your life when you met and fell in love with a cop?"

Camden smiled. "I've known from that first moment that Elijah would breathe life into my world. I didn't think he'd have to actually draw his service weapon to protect me, but I've always known I was safe with him."

"Now that the case is closed, and you have put away the leaders of the Path for their crimes, what comes next for you, ADA Warren? Will there be wedding bells, or maybe a promotion?"

Camden's heart swelled with the reporter's question. "If I'm lucky, both," Camden answered quickly. "Although Elijah and I have made nothing official at this moment, I do believe we're headed in that direction. Marriage, family, and building ties within the community are things our parents modeled for us. The Stephensons are probably the only family I know of who believes in truth, justice, and taking care of your community as strongly as my family does."

"That's saying a lot, considering your father is the chief judge of the New York Court of Appeals."

"I know." Camden laughed. "But it's true. I don't know who got away with less as a kid, me as the judge's son, or Elijah as the cop's. Service, it's part of who we are at our core."

"Judge Warren must be thrilled to know his son has made such a solid choice in a love interest."

Camden thought of the rage that might nearly choke his father when this interview aired. "I'm not sure happy is a strong enough word to describe what my father feels about Elijah and me. But you know how dads are when it comes to their sons."

"So, you've given us a little peek into your personal future. What about your professional one? What does a win like this mean for you? Are you next in line for the position of district attorney of the borough of Brooklyn?"

Camden turned again to the camera. "Well, I hadn't planned to announce anything, but since you're putting me on the spot, I may as well. I am throwing my hat into the political arena and running as a candidate for the office of the district attorney of Kings County."

"You heard the exclusive here on the *News at Six*. Not only is ADA Warren in love with a man who loves justice as much as he does, but he's also campaigning to be the next DA of Brooklyn. Nothing is impossible when you're fighting on the side of justice both on and off the battlefield. Thank you, ADA Warren. Thank you, Captain Searlington. And thank you, Lieutenant Stephenson, wherever you are tonight."

ELIJAH sat still, frozen by the affection he'd just witnessed from both Captain Searlington and the man he loved. "You all right, son?"

Elijah looked down at his mother, unsure of how to answer her, so he nodded. His father leaned forward to catch his gaze. "What the hell was that all about?"

Elijah's lips trembled before he spoke. "That was Camden saving my career, this family, and our relationship all at the same time. That was also my captain making it almost impossible for IA to come for me over that bullshit complaint by the judge." Not to mention embellishing his involvement in the case. Elijah hadn't been part of the investigation. He'd simply hidden Camden, and even that he hadn't done all that well. He'd have to thank her for that later.

"It sorta made it seem like you two have been dating for five years, and that the judge knew about it?"

Elijah smiled at his sister-in-law's comment. "It does, Viv, doesn't it?" He shook his head as he replayed the interview over in his head. It was brilliant. In a few moments he'd matched the Stephenson family's integrity right up there with the Warrens'. If the judge came for Elijah's family now, he'd be painting an ugly mark on the Warren name too. Damn, Camden was smart.

Elijah stood up quickly, checking his pocket for his wallet and keys. "I'm gonna head out." Elijah gave a nod to his family and noticed the large grins the four of them were wearing. They all knew exactly where Elijah was going. To find his man.

He made it to the driver's side of his car before he heard a familiar voice call from behind him on the other side of the street.

"Excuse me, Lieutenant. I hope I'm not too late to accept your invitation to demolish your brother's winning record again?"

A smile spread across Elijah's face as he recognized the voice. The sound of it made his heart dance with excitement. He took a deep breath before he turned around, trying to calm some of the giddiness threatening to burst through him. As soon as he saw Camden walking toward him from across the street, his smile broadened. "I just served them dinner. After they finish eating, they'll be ready to start."

Camden stepped in front of him. The woodsy scent of Camden's cologne tickled the night air. "What are you doing here, Camden? I thought you decided to bounce?" That last part was supposed to sound serious. Instead, the permanent smile on his face coupled with the bubble of laughter that escaped his lips kept Elijah from presenting his practiced, serious cop voice.

"I was, but then I thought about what kind of man did I want to be. Am I always going to let others, who claim to know better, bully me into things I don't want to do, or am I going to live my life on my own terms?" Camden gave a nonchalant shrug of his shoulder before answering his own questions. "The latter seemed more fun. So here I am."

"What about your dad? Your dad's not gonna be happy with you." Elijah was certain that was an understatement. From the few moments he'd spent in the judge's presence, he was sure that man was used to having his orders followed implicitly.

"He wasn't. My ears are still ringing from his rather loud and detailed phone call expressing his displeasure. But I told him that if he didn't back off from you and me, that I'd refuse to run for DA. He tried to threaten me with cutting me off, but that kind of doesn't work so well when I'm employed. I might not be able to keep you in luxury on a prosecutor's salary, but I could take you out for a slice of pizza every now and again. Would that work?"

Elijah stepped closer to him, kissing Camden slowly. He then broke the kiss, leaning back as he asked, "You sure you wanna play?"

Camden smiled, running his fingers through Elijah's locs as he touched his forehead to Elijah's. "I'm certain I want to partner with you every chance I get."

"We talking just for tonight?"

Camden joined their lips together again in a sweet kiss before saying, "For a lifetime if you'll have me."

"Forever and a day sounds better. You down?"

Elijah's heart damn near burst with happiness as he watched Camden smile and nod. "Forever and a day sounds better to me too, Lieutenant."

Coming in May 2019

⊙REAMSPUN DESIRES

Dreamspun Desires #81
Love Conventions by Morgan James

A happy ending worthy of a TV fantasy… in real life?

Ashland Wells is an actor of sci-fi cult fame but with little direction for the future when handsome grad student Remy Beaumont lands in his lap at a fan convention. Remy is everything Ash ever wanted and wished he could be—including out and proud. For twelve hours, they're the best of friends. But the convention ends, and Ash goes home knowing saying goodbye to Remy might be the biggest mistake he's ever made.

A few months later, they're reunited on a new production—Ash as an actor, Remy a writer—and though Ash doesn't plan to make the same mistake twice, being with Remy means going public about being gay. He's not sure that's a risk he—or his career—can handle, no matter how great the temptation.

If only they could write themselves the romantic happily ever after they both need.

Dreamspun Desires #82
Redesigning Landry Bishop by Kim Fielding

Love never goes out of style.

Landry Bishop fled his tiny hometown and never looked back. Now his expertise in food, fashion, and décor has earned him all Hollywood's glittering perks. But with his husband deceased and his personal assistant quitting, Landry has nobody to rely on—and no one to help him indulge his secret cravings.

Jordan Stryker seems a dubious prospect as Landry's new PA. While Landry is self-controlled and formal, Jordan is casual and speaks his mind. He also has questionable fashion sense and limited kitchen skills. But as Landry soon realizes, Jordan has many attractive qualities too.

With a strong pull toward Jordan, new career opportunities on the horizon, and a persistent tug from family back home, Landry is in a quandary. He can advise others on how to make their lives special, but what should he do about his own?